Moishele and
the Flowerless Rosebush

Mauricio Wrots

Moishele and the Flowerless Rosebush

Translated by Adriana Jorge

1st Edition
POD

KBR
Greenville
2015

Publisher **Noga Sklar**
Translation **Adriana Jorge**
Text edition **KBR**
Cover design **KBR, based on a photo by Larence Shustak, 1960 (detail)**

ISBN: 978-0-692-48100-4

KBR Editora Digital
www.kbrdigital.com
www.facebook.com/kbrdigital
contact@kbrdigital.com
1|864|373.4528

FIC027000 - Fiction

Mauricio Wrots lives in Rio de Janeiro. He started his career as a journalist in the discontinued satirical newspaper called *O Pasquim*, becoming well-known due to his criticism directed at the military dictatorship. At Globo television he worked as a writer for a satirical show called "Satiricom." At the Educational channel in Rio de Janeiro he created and coordinated the program called "Tribunal da História" ("The Court of History"). He published the short stories book *A Relatividade da Infidelidade* (*The Relativism of Infidelity*). With *Moishele and the Flowerless Rosebush*, his first novel published by KBR, he had the opportunity to meet his Jewish roots.

Author's email: wrots@uol.com.br

TABLE OF CONTENTS

1. SAVED FROM THE WATERS

It was mid-May in 1938, the fifth year of Hitler's era.

Vicentina, a black woman, who was completely out of touch with the Nazi eruption, which would indirectly change her life, was pouring her heart out to a *pai de santo*.[1]

She has always been a maid, but as she got "knocked up," she was fired and moved to Zenilda's wooden shack until she could work again.

She kept on living there. Her boy was about to turn one. Tião, Zenilda's partner, wasn't so happy about it. According to him, charity had already been done and it was time for her to go, get a life and find another job.

However, a child in her arms would drastically reduce her chances. There's nothing bosses dislike more than the "child of the maid," either the ones who arrive with the mother or the ones to come. Wailing, pee and poop steal attention from work and break the silence. Once, she envied her grandmother, who had food and shelter during slavery, fifty years ago.

There was no other way.

First, she checked the houses nearby. She found nothing. Not even in a house with a sign: "Maid needed."

---

1 Portuguese, meaning the supreme authority of some Afro-Brazilian religions.

"No! Not with a kid!"

She heard these same words at all doors she knocked.

Homeless, with a bundle of clothes on her back and carrying the little one, what could she do? She wouldn't "throw him away," as many people suggested, nor leave him in one of these asylums, which are all the same.

The *pai de santo* was listening. But was he really listening? He seemed to be asleep. Finally, he opened his eyes, red from smoking a cigar, and said:

"My child, you must look for a house with a flowerless rosebush in the garden; and take the boy... take the boy... you've got psychic powers!"

That was all. She tried to get more information. It wasn't possible, because he had already broken the connection with the spiritual entity. All she got was that short message: "Look for a house with a flowerless rosebush."

But where was it? Vicentina knew what a rosebush was: "That plant with beautiful flowers and lots of thorns." *The weird part is that he told me to take the boy. He said it twice.*

His words didn't make a lot of sense, but she wouldn't doubt *preto-velho*,[2] the entity speaking through the *pai de santo*'s mouth.

She was advised to start looking for a job in Tijuca or Grajaú, districts in Rio de Janeiro, where rich people lived in two-story houses, families that were always in need of a cook, a cleaner or someone for all these services. She wasn't successful in Tijuca, she didn't find the flowerless rosebush. The next day, she took the streetcar to Grajaú, carrying her lunch box and the kid's bottle.

From time to time, they sat on the curb and had a snack. After that, they would knock from house to house, asking, "Need a maid?"

The answer was always the same: A head to toe look, focusing on the kid, a disgusted face and "No!" sometimes not

---

2 Portuguese, the spirit of an old African slave.

even verbalized. She uselessly walked around several streets that day, as she wasn't sure she would go back there. Exhausted, she was getting discouraged about looking for such "flowerless rosebush."

Some people even wanted to take her kid. "I ain't gonna give him to you! Maybe I'll never see him again."

She could bear with Tião's angry face a bit longer. She joined forces and stubbornly kept looking for the mysterious rosebush.

However, a big, beautiful garden caught her attention. So many rosebushes… but all exuberantly blooming. She wouldn't waste her time knocking on this door, but the roses were so beautiful… white, yellow, red… She was fascinated. She wished she could work there, watering the flowers every day. *Too bad… this is not the house* preto-velho *talked about; it must have a flowerless rosebush. But knocking on the door wouldn't hurt, would it?* She needed to hurry because it was starting to rain. She knocked and clapped, but the house remained "silent."

She wasn't surprised. Humbly, she didn't delude herself; it was too much to ask for, to work in such a beautiful place, with white walls and big blue windows… It wasn't for her. She accepted the silent rejection; she wasn't aware that someone was observing her through a window gap. The person was testing her patience, hoping she would go away.

Faiga, the owner of that house, used to do that all the time. She would leave the poor creatures insisting until they got tired. She knew they were looking for a job. She was able to recognize them; they were always black, poor and ragged. And that one was carrying a child…

First raindrops started pouring down, getting stronger and stronger. In a residential area, without shelters and trees, there was no way she could protect herself. If she decided to run, she wouldn't have enough time, the boy would get wet. Then, she decided to ask for help:

"Ma'am, Ma'am!"

The rain was getting heavier and she screamed, "For

God's sake!" as she noticed there was someone in the house. If no one came out, she would break into that or any other house. She was desperate, after all, she couldn't allow her kid to get soaked and perhaps develop a serious disease.

Suddenly, however, the heavy raindrops stopped pouring on her head. Vicentina looked up and could see that a big umbrella was protecting her. A thin, tall and very white gentleman, with a black cap on the top of his head, was looking at her and smiling. Next, he opened the iron gate and they got into the house. She looked the man in the eye and knew she could trust him. She thought, without knowing why, that the place could be the one she was looking for. *But what about the flowerless rosebush?*

There, all roses were blooming! She was wondering: *Was the* pai de santo *wrong? Was it really "a flowerless rosebush" that he heard from the entity?*

The man with a *kippah*[3] was Mendel Rosenstrauch, a Jew from Ostrow, a tiny city in Poland.

With an apprehensive look in her eyes, Faiga powerlessly followed them to the bottom of the staircase. Mendel accommodated the woman on a sofa and asked his wife, who came quickly, looking surprised, to bring them some food. Faiga was already familiar with her husband's generosity outbreaks and she was sure that, as soon as the rain stopped, the unfortunate woman would leave. She brought them a plentiful meal, picking up everything available in the fridge: milk, cake, orange juice, cheese and even some leftover *gefilte fish*.[4] She also decided to pack some food and clothes for the poor woman. She thought that, acting that way, she could say that the practice of *Tzedakah*[5] had been done.

Mendel didn't make any questions. He made Vicentina feel at ease. Silently, he helped her handling the small plates and cutlery. Faiga also helped, wishing they would finish the meal

---

3 Religious garment, skullcap worn by Jews.
4 Fish balls.
5 Hebrew word for the acts we call "charity" in English.

quickly; she was bothered by the attention her husband would give to strangers. But when she saw him feeding the "nigger's" son, she panicked.

She had her own reasons…

2. MENDEL AND FAIGA

They met on the ship that brought them from Europe to Brazil, in the 1920's. They got married a few weeks after their arrival.

Goldsmith, with deep expertise in the jewelry industry, Mendel was luckier than most of his patricians, some without a profession, others ordinary tailors starting new lives, selling fabrics on the outskirts of the city, then the Capital of the Republic. In a few years, Mendel progressed financially and bought a house in an aristocratic neighborhood in Rio de Janeiro, called Grajaú.

They didn't have children, and Faiga's infertility, attested by many doctors, turned her into a bitter woman. Constantly, the threats of the old Jewish law, which authorizes to repudiate an infertile wife, allegorically crossed her mind; moreover, in her case, that would hurt a lot, because Mendel really liked kids.

Faiga didn't show her frustration, on the contrary, she acted as nothing was sentimentally missing in her marital relationship. It was somewhat true, but she used to test her husband's affection. Her insecurity was a second nature, mingled with a comprehensive feeling of guilt: The Jewish mother, a *Yiddishe mama*, has always been a myth, exalted even in famous songs and subject of affectionate and popular satires. Vigilant and possessive, she felt threatened by the presence of the woman and the boy. She couldn't wait for them to leave.

Vicentina was quiet. Starving, her gestures were pretty much related to her mouth and her kid's little mouth. Mendel placed the kid on his lap and grimaced. The boy laughed out loud.

Faiga, nervous, went to the kitchen to have some water sweetened with sugar. She was only able to observe, as she was fighting a battle without weapons in her hands. In that Jewish house, tacitly, the authority didn't belong to the woman, who didn't have a say; she didn't even try, after all, she wasn't a *Yiddishe mama*. She used to hold her tears every time she attended a *bris*[6] or a *bar mitzvah*.[7] In these occasions she observed her husband's face, and was certain he had on his mind that he would never see the *bris* or *bar mitzvah* of his own child. The continuity of the Rosenstrauch's family depended on Yacov, Mendel's youngest brother, who emigrated from Poland to Germany. Newlywed, he owned a small jewelry shop in Berlin, a dowry given by the father of the bride.

As Faiga returned from the kitchen, she shuddered at what she saw. She knew she was fighting a losing battle. The boy was already pulling her husband's short beard and he seemed to be enjoying, as he was laughing out loud. As the downpour was getting noisier, Mendel, excited, lifted the boy and said:

"*Moishele*,[8] Moishele!"

Noticing his wife's perplexity, he added:

"Moishele! Saved from the waters! Just imagine being caught up in the downpour outside! You were saved, not by an Egyptian princess, but by a humble Polish Jew, not by a floating straw basket, but by my old umbrella!"

Vicentina, recovered from hunger, spoke for the first time:

"Sorry for the hassle! Thank you for the food. As soon as the rain diminishes, I'll leave. I thought you were looking for a maid, but everything is so tidy!"

---

6 The ceremony of male circumcision.

7 A coming-of-age ceremony in the Jewish religion when a boy turns thirteen.

8 Diminutive of Moses, "Moishe" in Yiddish.

She looked at Faiga: "Ma'am, you must have two or more maids, my *pai de santo* must be wrong!"

"*Pai de santo?*" asked Mendel, sounding curious.

Living in Brazil for many years, Mendel had the chance to meet people of all religious beliefs. He was used to the Brazilian syncretism and was a Kabbalist himself, free from esoteric discriminations, curious about Vicentina's comments concerning the oracle of *Umbanda*.[9]

She told him: "I went to see him because I'm desperate, I can't find a job; the mistresses see the kid with me and do not even bother to answer my pleas, some people even want to keep my boy, but I won't give him away, no way. God forbid! I would never see him again! Then, I explained the whole situation to the *pai de santo*. He puffed on a cigar, took some time and said, using these very words: 'My child, you must look for a house with a flowerless rosebush in the garden.' That's the reason I knocked on your door."

Faiga felt encouraged by her words, and quickly said:

"Well, there are no flowerless rosebushes here. They're all blooming!"

"You're right, Ma'am. I knocked on the wrong house."

Faiga breathed a sigh of relief. Vicentina kept speaking:

"But when I saw all those rosebushes, I thought: Did I really hear the *pai de santo*'s words correctly? Perhaps he said 'a flowerful rosebush?' Dumb me. I wanted to stay here, where I could see such beauty daily, that's the reason I kept knocking on your door, until the rain started, forgive me, Ma'am."

Faiga thought she could turn an almost lost battle into an unexpected victory, and, being very friendly, she encouraged Vicentina:

"Don't give up! You'll find the right house, the one the man told you about, the one with a flowerless rosebush."

"Well, I guess the rain stopped," said the poor woman.

Hastily, Faiga helped her with the bundles, but avoided

---

9 Portuguese, an Afro-Brazilian religion.

holding the kid. She told her husband, in Yiddish, that Vicentina was a *mishiguene cop*, "crazy in the head," relating to the story of the flowerless rosebush.

Mendel, however, was a scholar of Kabbalah. He listened very carefully to the story the unfortunate woman was telling, including her useless and strenuous pilgrimage from door to door. He tried to interpret the words of the *preto-velho* embodied by the *pai de santo*. After a long period of meditation, he held Vicentina's hand, and, in a soft tone, told her:

"You no longer need to look for that house, because this is the house!"

What reasons would Mendel have to welcome Vicentina? They didn't need a maid, as they had a daily cleaner who was able to cope with the service. Actually, the couple didn't hire workers with long-term contracts, sleeping over, because they couldn't get used to it.

Why would Mendel hire Vicentina? And, on top of all, carrying a child? Faiga, heartbroken, figured that, perhaps, pity influenced his soft heart. She avoided contact with kids, something that used to trigger a distressing and uncontrollable wave of suppressed maternal feeling. *And now, how will things be?*

Mendel kept to himself the real reason concerning his decision. As a mystical person, he was able to understand the meaning of the "flowerless rosebush" Vicentina couldn't find in any garden. On the contrary, and due to specific circumstances, she knocked on a door with a garden full of blooming roses; she wasn't aware she had knocked on the right door, but Mendel, somehow, knew it was the right place. Why? Because he respected the former slaves' beliefs and was delighted at the subtle craftiness of the orishas.[10] This was the house of the "Rosenstrauch," their family name meaning "rosebush." They were a couple without kids, so, he and his wife would be the "flowerless rosebush," which, in mysterious ways, the *pai de santo* asked Vicentina to look for.

In Poland, before the racial harassment, the Jews had

---

10 African entities representing the forces of nature.

constantly faced religious persecution. They were accused of being the "Deicide People," the Christ-killers. During the Holy Week, their parents wouldn't let them play outside, because it was dangerous to be seen by fanatical Christians. For that reason, Mendel became a free-spirited man, and he used to compare the harassment against the African Spiritism to the one he had seen and felt in his native land.

He didn't fantasize meeting Vicentina, he wouldn't go that far, it wasn't about fate bringing him a son in the arms of his future maid. Maids come and go. But there was a touch of *Allan Kardec*[11] in his empirical ecumenism, "There are no coincidences!"

He analyzed the metaphysical meaning of the facts. *What could possibly have brought that mother and her son to my door? Was she only looking for a job?* There was something else concerning her arrival and the flowerless rosebush enigma, it could not be all. *There was something... but what?*

Only time could bring that answer.

Faiga, hiding her disappointment, accommodated them in a room attached to the kitchen. Her intention was to "confine" them in the laundry area, avoiding as much as possible their presence in other rooms. She would give specific orders and keep contact with them to a minimum. She had never had a maid, but, in fact, her real concern was related to the boy. She feared Mendel would get too close, keeping alive her latent guilt of being infertile.

She instructed Vicentina to keep her son in the room and never take him to other places in the house. He could play in the big wooded backyard, though. She acted in a preventive way. She took all possible precautions in order to overlook their presence in their lives, and she would quickly find any excuse to fire Vicentina.

"I don't want to see this boy around the house! Don't let him bother my husband!"

---

11 French educator, considered the father of Spiritism.

Faiga's orders worked well, but just for a while. Actually, only for a few hours. As much as we try to control the meanderings of life, the unexpected can discredit any caution.

Vicentina arrived on a Friday afternoon, right before the Sabbath, the Jewish weekly day of rest, which starts after the sunset, when the first star shows up. Then, the Jews stop their activities and start preparing for dinner. The Jewish woman is honored with few religious obligations, but during the Sabbath she is the "ritual queen": With a veil covering her head, she is responsible for lighting the candles and, moving her hands around the flames, reciting the divine blessing.

That night, however, in front of the well-set table, with nicely prepared *kosher*[12] food, during the candle lighting blessing, Faiga, side glancing, saw two amazed little eyes contemplating her in the back hallway.

It was the boy. He sneaked out, as his mother was distracted lighting a candle stub to thank Iemanjá[13] for the received grace. After seeing Vicentina's candle stub, the boy was attracted to the magnificent brightness of the long candles in shining silver chandeliers, and, crawling in a straight line, ended up in the living room where the ceremony was taking place.

With great difficulty, Faiga carried on a prayer. It was her big moment in the week, the wife in front of the husband asking for the heavenly blessings, the table cloth perfectly white, the silver cutlery shining, plenty of traditional dishes, prepared according to her husband's taste. And all would go down the drain on account of that very short intruder, who was sitting on the floor with a pacifier in his mouth. She was ready to take him away when Mendel saw him, and heartily greeted him:

"Moishele! Look who is here, Faiga! We have a guest!"

He stepped up to the boy and picked him up; then, he walked back to the table and put a piece of *challah*[14] in his "little guest's" mouth.

---

12 Food prepared according to Jewish dietary laws.
13 Female African deity.
14 Traditional Jewish egg-braided bread.

Faiga, paralyzed, almost fainted, needed to take her tranquilizer. She couldn't imagine something like this was even possible. For her, it was a desecration. The following day, she even thought about consulting a Rabbi in order to find out if Mendel was offending the Jewish law as he admitted a *goy*[15] at the table during the Sabbath. If necessary, that's what she would do.

Her friends were outraged when she told them her drama: The maid's son has stolen all the attention that used to be exclusively hers. They suggested firing Vicentina while Mendel was at work, giving him any excuse, including saying that she had quit.

Faiga began acting with premeditated calmness. When Mendel brought Moishele some toys, she even picked a rattle and, smiling, shook it in front of the kid. Naturally, she asked Vicentina to serve breakfast; she didn't want Mendel to attribute the planned dismissal to a poor treatment from her mistress. She had already set the day to fire her: It would happen on Thursday, a day before the beginning of the next Sabbath. The little brat wouldn't steal Mendel's attention any longer.

However, on Wednesday, a letter arrived from Germany. It was from Yacov, Mendel's brother, asking for information about Brazilian gemstones. He said he had been optimistic about the situation of the Jews in the country, concerning the Nazi persecution, believing the situation would get better soon. In the letter, he also sent a photograph of him and his wife in front of his shop. Mendel was holding it as Vicentina came closer, bringing a tray with milk and a coffee pot. Her eyes casually met the picture, and something unexplainable happened. From that moment on, that house would never be the same.

"It's my brother and his wife," said Mendel.

Vicentina placed the tray on the table. She got the photograph, brought it closer to her face, and suddenly went into a sort of trance. Her boss, who thought she was having an epileptic attack and was slowly recovering, quickly helped her. Faiga

---

15 Foreign, non-Jew.

brought her some water, anticipating more hassle and delay concerning her plan.

"What happened, my child? Do you want me to call a doctor?" asked Mendel.

"No. It's not necessary. I'm not sick. It was something else. I'm not sure I should tell you. You might think I'm nuts."

"Don't worry. You can trust me. Tell me what happened."

"That picture of your brother and his wife..."

"What about it?"

"I saw something horrible!"

Faiga couldn't understand what was going on. She could only think about getting rid of that burden as soon as possible.

Mendel insisted:

"Tell me! What have you seen?"

Vicentina, shyly, said she had had a vision when she looked at both of them in the picture.

"A vision? What vision?"

"Something really bad. I'm not sure I should tell you!"

"You can tell me. Don't be afraid."

"Both were on the floor, 'all bloodied', covered in broken glass, and around them there were some really violent men."

Surprisingly to his wife, Mendel didn't interrupt the narrative.

"What men? What type of people?"

"Men in uniform, with an armband."

Vicentina picked the envelope of the letter, looked around the stamp and pointed:

"An armband like the one this man is using!"

It was a swastika on Hitler's arm.

Impressed, Mendel got the envelope and the picture. Without saying a word, he went to the prayer room and asked for protection for his brother and sister-in-law. He knew, of course, that, through the Nuremberg Laws, the Nazi persecution had already removed the citizenship of the Jews, banned interracial marriages, the right to public offices, deals with Aryans and big industrial and commercial businesses. The infringement of physical integrity wasn't officially declared, but a good number of Jews didn't want to be around to witness the Third Reich's next step, and even losing 70% of their assets they struggled for an exit visa.

Many others, however, including Mendel's brother, didn't believe Hitler would last, and remained in Germany. *Was Vicentina's vision a warning? Would the next step of the Nazis include physical aggression or anything even worse?*

How should a European, practitioner of an ancient religion, face the premonition of an ordinary and illiterate maid, practitioner of a sidelined Spiritism which was even facing Police persecution? Mendel, on the other hand, shouldn't forget that, throughout the centuries, his people had been through many and recurring massacres, the *pogroms*.

Believing or not in something that could be a warning had become a troubling dilemma. If he were serious about it, or at least accepted the idea of a possible tragedy, he would have to do something. He wouldn't be able to forgive himself if Vicentina were right. And, as the Jews normally do, he wouldn't take any decision before a long meditation. He needed to strengthen his conviction.

Hesitant, he kept meditating. Should he simply ignore it? What if the Reich decided to stop playing cat and mouse and took extreme measures? How could he live with such guilt? Concerning these topics, he wasn't a practical man. He was trying to avoid a future painful regret. Advised by friends, he went to several *terreiros*[16] and consulted other *pais de santo*. He showed them his brother's letter, the picture and the envelope, besides asking about Vicentina's vision.

The incorporated entities didn't predict anything bad, on the contrary, the *babal*orishas[17] told him not to worry, saying that his brother was well and not at risk and that Vicentina's vision was a result of an undeveloped mediumship.

---

16 Houses of worship of some Afro-Brazilian religions, meaning "plot of land."

17 The high authorities in *terreiros*.

This pilgrimage to many mediunic centers, with African drums, clouds of cigar smoke and the smell of *cachaça*,[18] somehow made him feel calmer, and he concluded it wasn't an emergency. Thousands of miles away, how could she had seen something that didn't even happen? Something that wasn't even based on a rumor, such as the case in Eastern Europe, where the arrival of *Cossack*[19] killers was expected? Had he not listened to the words of the major *umbandistas*?[20] Has he not talked to Anastacio? Has he not consulted Ciata and many others? Why should he feel such affliction? All based on a delirium that, perhaps, was simply an epileptic attack, or, who knows, a trick to impress him and gain some kind of advantage.

Mendel settled down, forgot the incident and returned to his daily routine. But then he had a dream: In a *terreiro* of *Umbanda*, he heard his brother's life was at risk, and he should move heaven and earth to save him. The very unusual fact was, however, that the *pai de santo* wasn't an *umbandista*, but the old Rabbi Shlomo, the most respected Rabbi in his region in Poland, who, wearing his worn-out black overcoat, was smoking a thick cigar and drinking shots of *cachaça*. He woke up breathless, scaring his wife.

He told her his dream, but Faiga couldn't hide her disdain:

"The Holy Rabbi Shlomo? Smoking a cigar and drinking *cachaça* in a *terreiro*?" Laughing out loud, she got up and went to the kitchen to prepare breakfast.

Mendel felt alone in his ridiculous anxiety. He tried to be rational, but, through a mind mechanism, the superstition was becoming a premonition.

The following day, he went to Praça Onze, a square and meeting point for the Jewish immigrants in Rio de Janeiro, where he was expecting to get nothing more than disbelief and irony: A flowerless rosebush, a maid's vision, the brother's

18 Brazilian distilled spirit made from sugarcane.
19 People from Southern European Russia and adjacent parts of Asia.
20 Practitioners of *Umbanda*.

picture, the letter, the stamp, the Nazi aggression... who could possibly take him seriously?

The first person he talked to was Simon Wainberg, *a priori* a terrible advisor, an intellectual communist who didn't even attend the synagogue. He met him at a coffee shop, dipping buttered bread into a cup of latte. But the communist listened attentively to the whole story and showed real interest.

"So, what do you think?" asked Mendel, after telling the whole story, from Vicentina's arrival to her trance while looking at Yacov's picture.

His friend was quiet and thoughtful, and even laid aside his overflowing piece of bread. Then, looking deep into Mendel's eyes, the materialistic Simon Wainberg expressed his unexpected opinion:

"Mendel, everything seems so clear. This black woman must be fulfilling a spiritual mission. Or two. She brought a child to your home, and this will make your life better, happier, as you don't have kids. And what she saw in the picture, the slaughter of your brother and his wife, shows what, sooner or later, the Nazis will do to the Jews in Germany. Everyone who's aware of our history knows quite well how these things start: The ones who 'smell' disgrace in time will be able to escape, but the optimistic... She must have a very powerful orisha, it's impossible to disregard a warning like that. Mendel, you must find a way to take them out of there."

And he made a confession:

"Now and then, I go to a *terreiro*," he unbuttoned his shirt collar and showed Mendel a golden chain with two stars, a five-pointed and a six-pointed, representing the Star of *Umbanda* and the Star of David, respectively.

Amazed by the atheist-communist-*umbandista*'s words, Mendel thought it was no longer necessary to look for another source. If even a literate, politicized "red Jew" endorsed Vicentina's message, it was time to take action. Time was of essence, all of a sudden, everything could change concerning Hitler's anti-Semitic regime.

The bad feeling persisted, but he was facing another problem: How could he convince his brother to leave Germany and come to Brazil?

There was, of course, a set of racial restrictive laws, professional and commercial, imposed by the Nazi regime. But the complacent Yacov, answering Mendel's first letter, wrote: "I'm not, and I don't intend to be, a public officer, I don't intend to teach, so, for now, I keep living with my business; what else could the Nazis do to harm us?" Yacov, undoubtedly, was one of those naive optimistics Simon Wainberg mentioned.

Mendel decided to bring his brother to Brazil at all costs. His memory of the old massacres reinforced his willingness. In Poland and Russia, things had been similar to that, normally coming as a "surprise." He had read parts of *Mein Kampf*[21] in an Jewish newspaper. It wasn't the time to think about the saddle, the most important was saving the horse. But according to Yacov, there were no visible threats, so how could Mendel convince him he was at risk? Still enjoying his honeymoon, being an established businessman for the first time, how could Mendel tell him "Drop everything, sell your business at any price, save your life, save your wife's life, it's the advice of Vicentina, my maid, who had a vision and pointed out the stamp with a swastika..."

Yacov would laugh, thinking his "Brazilian" brother was nuts, perhaps a victim of some tropical fever.

Mendel didn't know why, but he felt he was in a race against time. He couldn't say when, but something, without any logic, was telling him a terrible thing was about to happen. Now, it was a matter of life and death, something much more complicated than a premonition. He would do whatever he could to convince Yacov, even against his will. He would come up with a lie; after all, it was about saving their lives.

He wasn't sure how he would do that. Yacov wouldn't

---

21 HITLER, Adolf. *My Struggle*. Germany: editor Rudolf Hess, 1925/26. Autobiographical manifesto by Hitler, outlining his political ideas and plans for Germany.

be satisfied with simple words on a piece of paper promising him the world in the tropical El Dorado. He needed a strong argument, commercially powerful. Or, at least, seeming big and serious...

He spent the following week feeling worried. During his sleepless nights, he thought about the letter he would send to Germany. He wouldn't be able to convince his brother with a message allowing many inquiries. He needed to be incisive, words such as "perhaps," "when" and "how" weren't permitted... At this point, an exchange of correspondence could be lethal, meaning the waste of precious time. How much time was left?

3. Mendel's Argument

The great idea, or rather, the great "lie," came to him on a Sunday, at an amusement park called Quinta da Boa Vista, traditional family activity at the time, while he was passing by a photography stall, where the photographer, through a photo montage, placed the clients' pictures in an airplane cabin, flying over the clouds.

Mendel talked to Machado, the portraitist, and, paying well, hired his services for an unusual task, a very ingenious plan that would touch Yacov's weakness. He paid for half of the service in advance and set all the details. The next day, wearing his best suit, Mendel placed himself next to the biggest and most luxurious jewelry shop on Ouvidor Street. Looking serious, he posed as the owner, and, on the other side of the street, Machado photographed the scene, quickly, as someone from the store could show up. Then, it was necessary to develop the photographic plate with an adjustment required by Mendel: Machado should scrape off the original name of the jewelry shop and place an assumed name: "ROSENSTRAUCH BROTHERS, JEWELLERS."

The montage was so perfect that, for a few seconds, Mendel felt like the real owner of the establishment. The brightness of a sunny day even allowed the mixed showcase within the shop window to be seen.

Mendel talked to no one about his plan, not even his wife. After all, they would probably doubt his clarity. He would send a letter to Germany, telling Yacov about the acquisition of the jewelry shop, saying he hadn't mentioned anything because it was something uncertain. They would become partners, as already written on the shop window. He hoped his brother would bite the bait and be courageous enough to sell his small business, even at a loss.

It was all a fantasy, of course, but Mendel considered it a necessary lie. Moved by the supernatural message, he was sure that Yacov was at risk and that the Nuremberg Nazi Laws, revoking the citizenship of the Jews, were just an appetizer considering what was to come, even though The Olympics Games in Germany, in 1936, temporarily softened the persecution, conveying the false impression that the worst had already happened. His brother's reaction after arriving in Brazil, and becoming aware of the farce, was a problem to be solved later. At that moment, what really mattered was saving those lives from a threat that he, in Brazil, felt closer than those living in the heart of the Third Reich.

Mendel also included in the letter some pictures of downtown Rio de Janeiro, with its Europeanized streets and avenues, showing his brother that he wouldn't arrive in the middle of a jungle, with snakes and naked Indians.

The letter arrived in Berlin in the beginning of July 1938. Looking at the picture of "his" jewelry shop in Brazil, with a great shop window full of showcases, and noticing his brother's and the bystanders' elegance, Yacov got really excited. He shared his excitement with his wife and they discussed the pros and cons. According to the Nazi laws, leaving Berlin basically meant losing your accumulated capital, that is to say, the property and the goods which assured your survival. The Reich imposed legitimate limitations, absurd onerous conditions for the Jews who decided to leave, forcing them to sell their assets at a great loss.

Another drawback included getting exit visas in Germany and entry visas in Brazil, besides the evil German bureaucracy concerning anything related to the Semites. However, Mendel had added a PS in the letter, saying that Yacov just needed to agree, and he, Mendel, would be responsible for enabling the trip.

Up to that moment, Yacov had endured with resignation all the prohibitions imposed by the regime, some highly ridiculous, such as visiting the Zoo, a privilege allowed only to Aryans. Yacov disdained: "I can do great without those animals!" Nevertheless, he felt sorry for leaving his beautiful city. He couldn't understand the reason for such rush; after all, Hitler wasn't "that Pharaoh who ordered the slaughter of innocent people."

Mendel insisted on an immediate answer. Yacov tried to resist, but he was concerned about his brother finding another partner. Hesitant, he didn't know he was dancing over an abyss: "Haven't the Nazis done enough against us? What else can they do? *Pogroms...* massacres... belong to the past, in Russia, in Ukraine, in Poland, not in a modern Western world. We are in Berlin, in 1938." His survival instinct was not that good.

He kept postponing an answer. He carefully listened to his wife's relatives, born in Germany, other businessmen and friends. *Moreover, at the slightest sign of risk, I could return to Poland, my home country, very close and safe*, he thought. Yacov's wife's family didn't welcome the idea of leaving. Would she, Erika, a native of Berlin, be able to live in the "Brazilian jungle?" And what about Yacov, an assimilated Pole; would he resist living as a fish out of water in such exotic and faraway place? It was a dilemma.

He could go on living without the citizenship, without the Zoo, without the public offices and, of course, without having sex with an Aryan woman, a criminal act that could even end up in death penalty. "All these have always been a luxury for our people."

But the picture of that magnificent jewelry shop on a major commercial street in Rio de Janeiro was stuck in his mind.

Some people Yacov talked to, on the contrary, envied his

luck, because the maximum they would get, through really hard working, was an exit visa to China, at the time, the only country that had kept its doors opened to the Jews.

A far more serious situation, commercially speaking, was losing the Aryan clients, as they were prohibited by law from entering the stores with a "J" in the shop front, making business impossible and forcing the Jews to sell low-priced jewelry. Fixing pieces was the only activity that ensured making some money — his thoughts were coming and going, as usual. On one hand, he could live well as his brother's partner in Rio de Janeiro; on the other hand, giving up the comfort of one of the best cities in Europe was painful.

In Brazil, Mendel was truly worried about the lack of news from his brother. He still believed in Vicentina's vision. Yacov should have quickly become aware he was at risk, but it didn't happen and time was flying. He decided to add another bait, an extra warranty: If nothing happened, if the Nazis let the Jews alone, even with so many restrictions, Yacov could go back to Germany free of any cost, and with a good capital given by him. And it was like that, using such attractive terms, that he finally convinced the couple.

The young couple faced the proposal as a leisure trip, without expenses and financial risk. They also requested all the privileges a luxury cruise could offer — they wouldn't travel on a ship full of scared immigrants — promptly accepted by Mendel, who noticed the time was going down the drain every time they exchanged letters.

They finally decided to come. Relieved, Mendel had another battle ahead: To get entry visas for the couple.

President Getúlio Vargas, at the time, was "flirting" with the Nazi, and had even authorized the extradition of a Jewish woman, Olga, Luís Carlos Prestes's wife,[22] who ended up being executed; and his "eugenic" immigration policy was object of secret circular letters sent to all consulates, prohibiting the entry

---

22 Controversial leader of the Brazilian Communist Party (PCB).

of the "unwelcome" — diplomatic euphemism concerning the Semite immigrants.

Mendel thought, even without concrete evidences, that something really bad would happen in Germany soon. He was aware of the Brazilian meanders and shortcuts, the so-called *jeitinho brasileiro*,[23] you just needed to know someone influential in the government and mobilize him or her in the necessary urgency. But he didn't know any politician, not even a council member. He needed to quickly find a way to bribe someone; many visas were bought behind the curtain. If he couldn't directly approach the big shot, he would have to do it through low-ranking, that means, looking for someone who knew someone and so on.

He hopefully thought about Matilde, an exuberant brunette, who used to buy expensive jewelry in his shop without a known source of income. Mendel, discreetly, knew the origin of such resources: They came from a member of the president's security guard, someone who was part of the group headed by the black man called Gregório Fortunato, Getúlio's "Black Angel," one of the most powerful characters of the Republic. Mendel decided to go to her house.

There, he unfolded the black velvet on the sofa. He selected the most beautiful bracelets, earrings, necklaces and golden rings. His client's eyes were shining, pretty much the same way the eyes of a *bandeirante*[24] shone when he found tourmalines and mistook them for emeralds. Amazed, she pressed her hands against her chest and choked on the words. She hesitated to try a ring or close a bracelet.

"This is all so beautiful, Mendel, but it's not for me! I've been your client for quite a while, you know how far I can go," Matilde reacted.

"Choose a bracelet, a ring and a pair of earrings," Mendel replied.

---

23 Portuguese, meaning "Brazilian way."
24 A Brazilian Explorer in the colonial era.

"Choose for what? I won't be able to buy them anyway."

"You don't have to pay. In return, I want you to do me a favor."

Matilde smiled in a playful way, somewhat malicious.

"What favor, Mendel?"

Mendel understood the joke.

"No, Matilde, that's not the case... The favor I need is from your friend Teixeira, the one from Gregório's group."

Matilde got excited:

"Teixeira will do anything I tell him to."

Mendel gave her the jewelry. In a few days, the Brazilian visas were issued, and, in Berlin, there were no difficulties, thanks to the good diplomatic relations between Brazil and Germany. When Yacov decided to travel, the racial laws and the anti-Semitic persecution hadn't reached their peak, there hadn't been bloodshed, except in isolated cases.

On board, the couple lived dream days. It was the sophisticated honeymoon they never had, in the first class of a comfortable transatlantic, and Yacov was promised a great and prestigious commercial position, as the partner of one of the main jewelry shops in Rio, according to his brother's letters.

He was somehow puzzled with Mendel's sudden progress. Being a non-established trader, he had suddenly reached such status in a short time, surprising his brother with the partnership proposal. *Things that happen in Brazil...* he thought, something similar to the stories he had heard about.

Just a few days before, in Berlin, his wife was standing in lines to get some rationed food. The ship, however, was an oasis. A cabin, fine wines, varied gastronomy and Strauss waltzes, pure Aryan treatment. On the high seas, during the journey, blended with the other passengers, Yacov even forgot about what it meant being a Jew. At a particular time, as a spontaneous reaction, he even responded to a greeting of an official, who, in a friendly way, stretched out his arm, using Hitler's greeting.

In the middle of the Atlantic, he didn't get news about international crises; actually, he didn't get any kind of news, and such isolation made him create an illusion that the world was a still lake. But while Yacov and Erika were waltzing in the majestic ballroom of the ship, under the splendor of gigantic crystal chandeliers, to the rhythm of the waltz "Tales from the Vienna Woods," at the dawn of the 10th of November 1938, in Berlin, the Viennese Joseph Goebbels was mobilizing the SA, the paramilitary group of the Nazi Party. He was planning retaliatory actions due to a murder in Paris, in which a young Jew killed an employee of the German Embassy.

While whirling and drinking champagne, the couple had no idea that, at the very moment, in Berlin, during the so-called "Night of Broken Glass" (*Kristallnacht*) — due to the shards of shattered glass on the floor reflecting the moonlight — broken glasses from the window of their jewelry shop would be lying in the middle of the street. Window panes of hundreds of other shops owned by the Jews would be shattered by the machiavellianly angered crowd, who extended the barbarism burning synagogues, killing, hurting and taking millions of members of their community to a prison in Dachau.

Not knowing about the attack, the couple arrived a few days later at the wharf in Rio de Janeiro, where Mendel was waiting for them. Deeply moved, the brothers hugged each other. But Yacov didn't have a clue why his brother was hugging him so tight. And why was he crying? They complained a lot about the hot weather. While they were in Mendel's 34 Ford going to Grajaú, the burning hood made them sweat in their European outfits. They glanced at each other, showing some regret; perhaps they wouldn't get used to that heat. If they could, they would return to the wharf and take the same ship back to Germany, but, soon, they would know it was no longer possible to set foot on German soil without being at risk of death.

They asked themselves: *Was it worth it coming to such inhospitable place, even considering a great financial advantage?* After being lodged and already rested from the trip, it was time to face the shock of reality. While they were having an afternoon snack, Yacov's feared question came up:

"When are we going to the jewelry shop?"

Erika, uneasy, already wanted to know, if it was the case, how they would go back, and gave her husband squinting, accusatory looks. Mendel, looking serious, observed the couple's naive ignorance: They weren't aware of the massacre in Berlin yet. He had not said anything.

He simply picked the newspapers of the Jewish press and gave them to Yacov. The atrocities of November 10th, which caused the death of 91 Jews, sent millions to Dachau concentration camp and burned and destroyed hundreds of synagogues, were the headlines on the first pages; the stores had been looted and the shop windows crashed, while the couple enjoyed the security and comfort of a transatlantic ship.

After reading the news about the gloomy dawn, Yacov cried. He thought about his loved ones there, such as Erika's parents, and he was sure that a new and even more terrible Hitlerism wave had started. He imagined the golden letters on his small shop window turned into uncountable pieces of broken glass. He was also aware that he had narrowly escaped the brutality against the Jews, which marked the beginning of the history of the Holocaust.

If Mendel hadn't insisted and proposed a partnership, he would have stayed in Berlin. He got goose bumps just by imagining where and how he would be. Germany was over for him. Slowly, he was adapting to the coup, and tried to get used to the surroundings. But, again, he asked about the jewelry shop.

It was the moment of truth. Mendel even rehearsed an apologetic tone, but he took courage and went straight to the point, without hesitating:

"Yacov, I want you to forgive me, but this jewelry shop doesn't exist. It was an argument I used to bring you and your wife to Brazil, to save you both from annihilation."

Yacov was reluctant to understand his explanation. He couldn't believe it. He thought Mendel was joking.

"Mendel, how could you come up with such a story? What about the picture you sent me?"

"It was a photo montage, I asked a professional to change the name on the shop window."

"You're mad, brother! Why such a lie?"

Mendel showed him, again, the headlines.

"To save your life, to keep you out of a concentration camp!"

Yacov was still confused.

"But no one knew about it! Not even me, who used to live in the Reich. How did you know about the *pogrom* in such advance? Is Mendel Rosenstrauch a prophet?"

Mendel wasn't sure about his answer. It would sound ridiculous for a newcomer from Germany, Einstein's homeland, to accept everything happened because of Vicentina, who, while serving breakfast, glimpsed a picture of the couple and had a vision in which both were being beaten. But he didn't evade his brother question, he wouldn't care if he laughed at him. Yacov was safe, and it was all that mattered.

"I'm not a prophet, but Vicentina is."

"And who is Vicentina? A woman with a crystal ball?"

"Nope! Vicentina is our maid, that woman you saw working in the kitchen. She belongs to a spiritualist lineage of African slaves, and some practitioners of this religion are clairvoyants. When she saw your picture, she got into a trance, and had a vision of you two lying on the floor, your bodies bleeding, covered in broken glass; and she pointed the armband with the swastika on the stamp of the letter, saying your aggressors were wearing it as well. Reading the newspapers, we know that it really happened to thousands of Jews, all staged by the Nazis under the pretext of revenging the murder of a German diplomat in Paris. Now, I ask you: How could she know that? What about the swastika? She had no idea these things even exist. She simply saw the man and the woman in the picture being slaughtered, and I didn't despise a warning coming from someone so humble, I couldn't be that arrogant; even facing my friends' mockery, I didn't give up taking you two out of there. And again I ask you: If it weren't for Vicentina, where would both of you be right now? Besides that, the Kabbalah teaches us not to despise certain signs, certain warnings, no matter where they come from."

Yacov was relieved that he wasn't taken by the vortex of the *Kristallnacht*, but he was frustrated because the jewelry shop in Brazil, which fed his dreams for a short time, didn't exist. He couldn't help admiring his brother's trick to bring him to the country, since he wouldn't have emigrated without that photo montage; and, if his ambition hadn't defeated his convenience, he would have kept living there, hoping the persecution would stop for a while, as it happened in 1936, during the Olympic Games in Berlin.

Without the possibility of returning, he had to adapt to the new place. The unbearable heat made him sweat all the time, forcing him to use equally unbearable fans, which made his wife complain because they messed her hair. He missed the time snow blocked his door and way. *It was so good to live in Berlin...*

Actually, Yacov thought the clairvoyant's story was also made up by Mendel. But he remained silent. Neither had he pictured himself selling rings, earrings, necklaces and golden chains in government agencies, the type of job that was waiting for him. He thought this work was somewhat humiliating, as he had been a small, but established trader in one of the biggest European capitals.

Two opposite poles determined his feelings towards Mendel: Consciously, he was grateful because he was saved from the hordes of Hitlerism; on the other hand, already out of risk, he still suffered due to the false commercial expectation, a good lie who broke his resistance and made him cross the ocean. He asked himself: *couldn't it have been done in a different way?* And he, himself, answered: *No! Without the picture of the shop I would have never come...*

Mendel didn't pressure him. Yacov was trying to adapt to the place and the weather, a hard task for someone who used to live in the cultured Berlin. It was completely different if compared to the immigrants from Poland, who, in most cases — including Mendel's —, came from remote regions where electricity was not common, the opportunities were very scarce and the anti-Semite tradition originated from centuries of Christianism. In Germany, from way back, the Enlightenment took the Jews out of the ghetto.

But Berlin should be forgotten. Germany was, now, Hitler's hatred. Erika wrote a letter to her relatives living in Buenos Aires — Argentina was prospering thanks to wheat exports and, mainly, to the meat. So, an invitation was made: Why don't you come to the Argentinean capital, known as the "Paris of South America"? When Yacov heard about a snowy region in Argentina, and saw pictures of ski tracks in Bariloche, he was very excited, and approved the idea.

They had spent only three months in Brazil, and decided to go. Erika was constantly feeling nauseous and a doctor's appointment cleared the doubt: She was pregnant. Only on the eve of their departure, the incredulous Yacov, appreciating the beauty of the rosebushes, meditated, still intrigued, about that mysterious and absurd story, thinking about the circumstances that had led mother and son to Mendel's house.

While "talking" to the rosebushes, with a grin, he repeated his own name: "Rosenstrauch." How could he possibly understand the enigma of that woman whom Mendel believed, not giving up until they were out of risk, a risk which, for being stubborn, neither Erika nor he wanted to face, even after listening to the *Führer's*[25] threatening speeches, or seeing the brown shirts — the Nazi shock troopers — passing by his door?

He shivered, while realizing that Vicentina, through intuition, hunch or revelation — it didn't really matter — saved not only the couple, but also the baby who was on the way. He finally gave up finding an explanation.

On the day of departure, Mendel would drive them to the wharf. But before leaving the house, while saying goodbye, under surprised looks, the quiet and unsociable Erika hugged Vicentina with tears in her eyes and kissed the boy in her arms.

---

25 German word for "leader", especially applied to Adolf Hitler (*der Führer*).

She took off her golden chain with a Star of David and put it on him.

Yacov and Erika traveled without knowing that Vicentina had had another vision, which she only told Mendel:

"Those men burned the lady's piano."

Mendel asked his sister-in-law if she used to have a piano, but he chose not to tell anything.

"Yes, I did! It's at my parent's house on Prinzregentenstrasse, I wish I had it here with me!"

It was one of the most aristocratic streets in Berlin.

What about the house? Did the vandals burn it too? Mendel was concerned about Erika's parents, but Vicentina didn't say anything about them. Months later, through a letter from his brother, he learned that the piano, the house and her parents had not escaped. The beautiful house was burned to the ground and her parents were taken to Dachau concentration camp.

In parallel, causing great concern, the fast increase of the actions against the Jews in Germany, anticipating even darker actions, made Mendel feel proud for not being arrogant and for believing the "Kabbalistic" message coming from a humble creature of esoteric creed. And it all happened because that day, in front of his house, he protected Moishele and Vicentina with his umbrella.

It was not a simple coincidence. If he had arrived later, he wouldn't have met them, he wouldn't have listened to the message about the flowerless rosebush, he wouldn't have hired Vicentina, she wouldn't have had the vision about the "Night of Broken Glass" and he wouldn't have saved his brother. From then on, Faiga gave in and accepted that Moishele and Mendel would make their own history.

4. MENDEL AND MOISHELE

Over time, Mendel and Moishele would be the protagonists of an unusual father and son love story. A simple look, with eyes wide-open, through which Mendel met the boy's little eyes, and Moishele's laughter on that first day, linked the abiding affection between the newcomer kid and the playful sexagenarian.

Consulting the Kabbalah, and analyzing point by point what had happened, including how he met the mother and the son in front of his house ready to get soaked, up to Vicentina's strange narrative in search of a flowerless rosebush, Mendel, a Mason, attributed to fate, conducted by the "Great Architect," the meeting that had saved his brother from hell. And guaranteed the continuity of his family's name, as Erika had had the baby she was expecting when she left Brazil, a boy.

"He who saves a single life, saves the world entire," says the *Talmud*.[26] Mendel also added that it wouldn't matter if it happened through a physically heroic act or through the involuntary mystic clairvoyance of an ordinary worker.

Mendel was a righteous man. Vicentina left the maid's room with Moishele and started using the guest room, empty since his brother left. A fair person, however, cannot be a hyp-

---

26 Hebrew, a large collection of writings, containing a full account of the civil and religious laws of the Jews.

ocrite. And he wasn't. A simple improvement concerning the treatment between masters and slaves had been a common episode. For that reason, Mendel told Vicentina she was no longer the maid and that she could live in his house with her son as long as she wished as a member of the family, and that she would receive an allowance. Vicentina thanked him crying, but, basically, begged him to continue as she was. She enjoyed domestic chores, and said they were good for her. She didn't find it fair contracting another maid. She accepted one or two privileges, including the permission to go to a *terreiro* every Friday night.

That way, Faiga and Mendel's home became Vicentina and Moishele's home, sheltering, for a long time, the coexistence between two religions. Faiga, who were terrified at the beginning, finally got used to the *Yoruba*[27] hymns coming from Vicentina's room. Sometimes, distracted, she found herself singing parts of them, what had caused great embarrassment. Once she was in the synagogue, with other women, and started distractedly humming a piece mentioning Iemanjá and Oxalá.[28]

Vicentina also got influenced. She really liked saying *Shalom*[29] and *Shabbat* whenever she could, without really understanding the meaning of the words. She thought it was the *saravá*[30] of the Jews.

Moishele had been sleeping with his mother, and Mendel bought him a cradle, and brought him a complete trousseau as well, besides rattles and little cloth animals. But it was the stroller that got everyone excited. The next day, with the kid in the stroller, he made his first visit to the little square in his neighborhood, where, proudly, he answered all the questions made by the neighbors sitting on benches.

27 A large ethno-linguistic *group* or *ethnic* nation in Africa.
28 Portuguese, African deity.
29 Hebrew word normally used as both a greeting and farewell, commonly translated as "peace."
30 Portuguese, word used by practitioners of some Afro-Brazilian religions, meaning "good luck."

"Who's that boy?" asked Rachel, a friend of the family.

"He's my son!" answered Mendel, smiling.

He knew that the simple fact of being "caught" by Rachel was a guarantee that, in a short period of time, the whole Jewish community would be commenting that a Jew from Grajaú had a son with his black maid.

There was a setback during the stroll: Moishele started to cry because he was hungry. It was bottle time, and Mendel was desperate as Moishele screamed louder. As an inexperienced dad, he hadn't brought anything. The crying was so powerful that caught the attention of a babysitter carrying a kid in a stroller. The solution was taking the "little friend's" bottle, as he only had two thirds of his meal.

The situation was enough to make Mendel study everything about mealtime and read all the material related to "Baby Care." He wasn't able, yet, to change diapers, but he was saved, again, by the babysitter who had "lent" him a bottle.

Mendel could hire a babysitter, but his desire to become a father, suppressed for many years, turned him into a father, a mother and a babysitter, all at the same time.

Faiga, defeated by the facts, no longer imposed her initial resistance. After all, she witnessed Mendel's struggle to bring his brother to Brazil after Vicentina's vision. How could she ignore such a great debt? She got used to sharing her attention, and, slowly, she was also becoming closer to the boy. The embarrassment took place while she spent time with her friends, who, constantly and maliciously, asked about Mendel's great affection for a *goy* kid. "Why hadn't they adopted a Jew child?" Faiga didn't dare telling the story about the letter from Germany, the maid's role and everything else. She only said that Mendel really liked children and grew fond of the maid's son, who hadn't been adopted, as his mom was raising him. The father had died as he jumped from a moving streetcar while going to work.

Mendel was ironic, saying it was a matter of affinity: "It's the meeting of two slave descendants, only centuries apart. My ancestors were freed in Egypt five thousand years ago, and his ancestors, in Brazil, were freed only fifty and something years ago."

Moishele's real name was Jorge. He was named after the Warrior Saint — Ogum, in *Umbanda*. Realizing his birthday was coming, Mendel decided to offer him a birthday party. Without any previous experience, he had asked Vicentina to bake a cake and prepare the snacks. He also asked Faiga to prepare potato *beigueles*[31] and *kosher varenikes*.[32] He was going to invite the kids from the neighborhood, including the ones from Jewish families. He told Vicentina she was free to invite whomever she wanted.

In the back porch, there was a big table and dozens of chairs, which were slowly taken by the guests – side by side, some orthodox Jews with a full beard, wearing their hats and black overcoats, and *umbandistas* wearing white clothes, necklaces and *patuás*.[33] On the table, in full harmony, the *beigueles* and *kosher varenikes* "shared" space with the "profane" Brazilian snacks prepared by Vicentina. A huge cake, with cream and coconut icing, with a single candle indicating the boy's age, proved to be a delicious unanimity, as the orthodox, consulting each other, couldn't remember, or didn't want to, any religious prohibition able to stop them from enjoying such "temptation."

Counting on Mendel's help, Moishele blow the candle with two little blows, actually spitting more than blowing. As usual, it was time to sing "Happy Birthday" and, not so usual, shouts of *Mazal Tov*[34] were led by Mendel. The beneficial purification rituals started and there was a lot of cigar smoke in the place, hurting a little the orthodoxes' eyes.

Mendel thought it was fair to give Vicentina some special attention, so he told the guests the whole story, from the moment she arrived at his house up to the fact, then speaking loud and clear, that, from Brazil, so far away, she was able to

---

31 Snacks of the traditional Jewish gastronomy.
32 Boiled dumpling stuffed with potato, cheese or other filling.
33 Various charms used by members of *Umbanda*.
34 Hebrew expression of "congratulations" or "best wishes."

defeat the Nazis killing frenzy, what, in fact, was understood only by a few. But the religious men, wearing black overcoats and hats, were moved by the happy end, and some felt sorry for not doing the same with their relatives, already taken by SS executioners. That way, the party went on, with Moishele under the protection of the orishas and wearing a golden *Aleph*[35] around his little neck. Also, as usual, the men and women in white took home little plates with the Brazilian snacks, besides, of course, pieces of cake. The religious men in black didn't refuse the *beigueles* and *varenikes* that were left.

In contrast with Vicentina's euphoria, Faiga was quiet, and somewhat sad. She almost didn't take part in the celebration. Whenever possible, under any pretext, she would leave the party and seek refuge in any isolated place, crying over her maternal impossibility.

Nevertheless, she was able to perform a great gesture by helping a homeless, who, from the street, stretched his arm over the wall: She got a little plate with *beigueles* and Brazilian snacks and placed it in the unexpected visitor's hand. For different reasons, it was, perhaps, the first time the homeless man had tasted such snacks — the unfortunate man had never seen a *beiguele*, and concerning the Brazilian snacks, although he had seen them daily through the bakery window, he couldn't afford the luxury of eating them without exceeding his "budget."

Faiga's social superiority was nothing compared to her psychological inferiority concerning Vicentina, whose boy reigned in her own house. Once again, she felt sorry for not agreeing with Mendel's idea of adopting a Jewish child. After becoming an adult, Mendel had no longer played with a child, and "being a child" again was doing him good.

An event that was far from tragic, and somehow comic, was Moishele's "kidnapping." A crook who used to live in the neighborhood saw Mendel getting into his house with the boy in the stroller, returning from a walk. The impressive house and

---

35 The first letter of the Hebrew alphabet.

the luxury stroller led him to believe that he could earn some money by taking the boy, the son of that very rich man. He told his two stooges all the details about the house. At a convenient time, determined by the informer, they jumped over the wall and broke into the house through an open window. Inside the house, they searched all rooms, but couldn't find the "owner's son." They scared Vicentina, who was washing clothes outside, and left without causing any harm.

Later, they came to terms with the crook; after all, they were at risk for nothing: The parents had left with the baby. In the house there was only the "son of the maid," with little aggregated commercial value.

After a while, Moishele called Mendel "daddy" for the first time. It happened when they were in the little square, passing by a cotton candy cart. Although it was somehow predictable, the Jew was so moved he could barely walk. Seeing such happy little face, he couldn't hold his tears, while the little boy, repeatedly, pointed at the seller. Both ended up smeared with snow sugar.

Mendel was concerned about his wife's reaction. In normal circumstances, she would be the "mommy," so he should be very careful not to upset her; after all, she still carried a great anguish that tormented her. It was necessary to give her some time. Who knows, after growing a bit more, Moishele would get used to having two mothers... He hoped it would happen naturally, and, now and then, he tried to find a reason to put the boy on Faiga's lap. On these occasions, he knew he could be bringing some relief to her suppressed maternal instinct, or, on the contrary, causing some kind of depression.

He wasn't very extroverted with the boy when Faiga was around; through restrained gestures and words, he tried not to hurt her, hoping that the first act of fondness would come from her, motivated by a smile or even a whining.

Faiga was born in Opatow, a small Polish town next to Lublin. Her father was a shoemaker, so she started working at a young age and became an excellent worker in a brush factory. During winter, she left work at dawn, walking on snow. Letters from friends convinced her father to send her to Brazil, where she would find enough support to start a new life, and get married. Parents felt brokenhearted by sending their children to such a far and "wild" land. Even though they got demystifying information, they didn't feel comfortable. They were still worried about their kids being hit by an arrow or bitten by a snake on Brazilian streets. But by sending them away, they were, without being aware, saving them from the Holocaust which was about to start.

Mendel had brought some diamonds stitched into his coat, which he kept on and buttoned during the whole trip, twenty-four hours a day. After arriving, properly advised by his compatriots, he turned the stones into capital and chose to work in the jewelry business, an art and technique that had been passed by his grandfather to his father and by his father to him.

He was amazed by the consumer market potential in Rio de Janeiro, at the time, the Federal Capital, with its congressmen, wives and lovers. Also, to his surprise, the civil service allowed him easy access to the government offices. His biggest joy, besides the commercial profit, was the excitement of his clients while he slowly unfolded the black velvet, displaying the jewelry made with his hands. Feeling that kind of "warmth" outside of his own community was something totally new to him, and, for that reason, in a short time, he was fond of the new land. After three years, he could buy a beautiful two-story house in the aristocratic district called Grajaú. Time, very generous, offered him all the material wealth, even a 34 Ford, a luxury for a few. But time didn't give him and his wife the child they have dreamed of since they got married.

At the age of three, Moishele started attending the synagogue with his "father." Mendel didn't introduce him to his religion, he simply placed a *kippah* on his head and let him be totally at ease. After listening many times, the boy memorized two or three words from some much repeated Jewish prayers. Mendel used to laugh a lot when, sometimes, he found the boy mechanically repeating, around the house, *baru atah, baru atah…*[36]

Every time he saw Mendel taking the *tallit*[37] from the drawer, he happily started saying: *baru atah, baru atah…*

Of course, a black kid in a synagogue generated lots of comments, but soon the pair came to be seen naturally. Some people even liked to tease Moishele, only to hear him saying: *baru atah, baru atah…*

Moishele, however, was free. Mendel didn't suggest anything that could lead him to a specific religious path, and also didn't oppose the fact that Vicentina normally took him to the *terreiro*, where the boy was in contact with a very different liturgy. Moishele, or Jorge, really liked the drums and the place, and missed them while in the synagogue.

As Faiga and Mendel communicated in Yiddish, Mendel enjoyed playing and teaching Moishele some Yiddish words, which were becoming incorporated into his rising vocabulary. He didn't miss the opportunity of showing Moishele many objects, telling him the names, and, didactically, asking him to repeat. As the years went by, Moishele became the only black person in town who could fluently speak the idiom of the *Ashkenazim*, Jews from Eastern Europe and Germany. He was growing up under the influence of two different cultures in the same house, one of Jewish nature, transmitted by Mendel, without proselytism, and another by Vicentina, who worshipped the orishas.

Talking to his friends, Mendel was frequently asked about the fact of having a *macumbeira*[38] at home. Many times, Faiga also brought up the topic related to such idolatry, somehow insinuating that the statues of Saint George and Iemanjá in Vicentina's room violated the rules of a Jewish home. Mendel

---

36 From the Hebrew prayer "Baruch Atah Adonai" ["Blessed are thou, Lord"].

37 Jewish prayer shawl.

38 Portuguese, a derogatory term used to describe a practitioner of an Afro-Brazilian religion.

had the answer on the tip of his tongue: "During centuries, and still nowadays, we have been persecuted due to our religion. We can't, ourselves, become the persecutors; after all, Vicentina's arrival provided us a true miracle, saving Yacov's life."

Always very moved, Mendel used to mention how Vicentina warned him about the threats to his brother, simply by looking at a picture. He had to respect a creed capable of that. He searched information about *Umbanda* and the orishas, and learned that Saint George was Ogum and Our Lady of the Immaculate Conception was Iemanjá. He also heard about many Jews who used to attend the *terreiros*.

One day, in October 1942, he asked Vicentina to take him to the *terreiro* she attended. Poland was under German occupation. In front of a *pai de santo* in trance, who seemed to be "far away" for a couple of minutes, immersed in lots of cigar smoke, he heard from him that his father's spirit was saying that his whole family had been slaughtered. Very nervous, he asked for details. He couldn't understand what was going on. As he believed his father was alive, it couldn't possibly be his spirit.

Suddenly, the *pai de santo's* voice changed. Mendel was frightened, as he noticed that a voice was speaking Yiddish. He almost fainted when he realized the voice was his father's, telling him that his whole family had been executed by the Germans, along with the whole Jewish population in the city. His father asked him to pray the *Kaddish*, the Jewish prayer in honor of the deceased.

When Mendel left the *terreiro* he was crying compulsively, he could barely speak. He got home shaking and febrile. Vicentina was trying to find out the reason for such pain, as she didn't know what the incorporated spirit told Mendel. Assisted by his wife, who had asked him what happened, he couldn't answer. He only mumbled: "My father..."

Until that day, although worried about the invasion in Poland, where his relatives used to live, he hadn't received any news about the annihilation. He thought they were all fine, even being aware that the country had been occupied by the Germans since 1939 and all communication had been cut off.

After a deep sleep, he could finally tell Faiga what happened in the *terreiro*. His wife couldn't help being ironic:

"This is all I need! The Jew Mendel, so religious, was at a *terreiro* and became ill because of what he heard from a *macumbeiro*..."

She tried to convince him of the opposite: "Such a misfortune? It can't be true, the Germans wouldn't kill all the Jews in the city, out of the blue. How come we didn't hear anything about it on the radio?"

Mendel kept believing the massacre took place. But, once again, he was worried: How could he tell the other Poles about it without sounding ridiculous? How could he explain that a *pai de santo* spoke Yiddish without being mocked?

Faiga tried to bring back his rationality. After all, not even the Jewish press had mentioned anything like that; only some news about persecutions, imprisonments, ghettos, but nothing like an annihilation.

Mendel couldn't forget Vicentina's vision, that saved his brother and his wife. He was sure his family had perished at Nazi hands. He tried to talk to the most prominent Jews in town, the ones with important connections, in search of news from Poland. None of them had heard about anything of such magnitude. The letters were no longer arriving, and nobody really knew what was going on over there.

Mendel remained tormented. He considered the collective execution consummated, but he was not capable of gathering a *minyan*[39] to pray the *Kaddish* requested by his father. Yet, he wouldn't give up. He was focused on an obligation that he alone had to fulfill. On a Friday, he arrived earlier at the synagogue and told the Rabbi the whole story.

All he got was a reprimand. The Rabbi accused him of

---

39 Hebrew, the quorum of ten Jewish adults required for certain religious obligations.

offending the *Torah*[40] and of worshiping the "Golden Calf" for going to such impure place. He recommended praying a lot, but said it would be better for him to pray by himself.

Mendel was depressed. He spent days in bed and wasn't eating. He refused to see a doctor. He didn't want to talk to anyone. During visits, he remained silent; his friends were shocked, with a feeling that Mendel was really sick. He was slowly languishing. He kept listening to the voice speaking Yiddish, asking him to say the prayer in honor of the deceased, but, without the *minyan*, blocked by the Rabbi, he couldn't do it.

In an afternoon, while Faiga was looking for a doctor, Vincetina entered his room and Mendel told her the reason of his "sickness": He had to pray for his father in the synagogue, as the father, himself, had asked him, through the *pai de santo*. But the Rabbi rejected any manifestation that took place in a *terreiro*, and accused him of offending his religion.

On that same night, Vicentina asked the orishas to alleviate Mendel's sorrow, because she was truly concerned about his health condition. The following morning, she rushed into Mendel's room to tell him a dream she had. An entity showed up and asked her to tell him to speak to the Rabbi again, and also tell him, the Rabbi, that he needed to pray for his father as well, as all his family had been killed by men in black uniforms with that armband.

"He will call me nuts and kick me out of the synagogue!" Mendel replied.

"The entity also said that "Ishmalt" was with a Christian neighbor and was doing fine," Vicentina added.

Mendel couldn't understand the meaning of "ishmalt." It didn't sound like a name, it sounded more like *schmaltz* — the Yiddish word for "melted animal fat," usually chicken fat, used for cooking.

Vicentina's message didn't make any sense, but that was her dream. "Ishmalt was fine."

---

40 From Hebrew, meaning "Jewish Written Law." Consists of the Five books of the Hebrew Bible — known to non-Jews as the "Old Testament."

He had many reasons to trust her, as, due to her clairvoyance, Yacov was safe, living in Argentina. *What about the* pai de santo *speaking Yiddish?* He had no doubts it was his father, asking him to pray the *Kaddish* in the synagogue. *Perhaps something similar had happened to the Rabbi's family.*

He got up and went to the synagogue. At that time, secretively, people were already saying that he wasn't right in the head, that he was *misheguene*.[41] The Rabbi asked him to sit down and let him talk, determined to devoutly listen to his delusions without interrupting, even pretending he was believing his words.

"Rabbi Meyer, sorry for bothering you again."

"No problem, Mendel, you don't bother me."

"I have a very important message to you."

"A message? From whom?"

"From an orisha who showed up in Vicentina's dream."

"Who is Vicentina?"

"She's my maid."

"And what is an orisha?"

"An *Umbanda* entity."

The Rabbi felt sorry for Mendel. If he had had any doubt about the rumors in the synagogue, unfortunately, at this point, he would have been sure they were correct. Penalized, he decided to give Mendel some attention before asking him to leave.

"Oh well, Mendel, tell me, what is the message?"

Mendel noticed the Rabbi was listening to him out of pity. He knew everybody was questioning his sanity, but he kept talking anyway:

"Forgive my audacity, but I think I have the obligation to tell you. The orisha that showed up in Vicentina's dream said that men in black uniform killed your whole family in Poland."

The Rabbi, that was calm and patient, suddenly stood up. Mendel had gone too far with his craziness. But he controlled himself, and asked Mendel to leave, as the message had been given.

---

41 Crazy, in Yiddish.

Mendel apologized again and said goodbye. But before leaving, he remembered to mention a detail:

"I don't know what it means, it's something really strange, but the orisha asked me to tell you that *shmaltz* was with the neighbor and was fine."

The Rabbi asked Mendel to repeat the message. After listening, for many times, that *shmaltz* was fine, he was copiously crying. With a deep sorrow, he said:

"Mendel, you can pray your father's *Kaddish*. I will arrange the *minyan* myself. I will pray for my father too."

At this point, the Rabbi was convinced his family was over.

They hugged each other, and Mendel left without understanding the Rabbi's sudden change in attitude, as he was unrepentant concerning his request. *What could have changed his mind, made him believe they were all dead?*

Mendel could never imagine, neither did the Rabbi told him, that he used to have a little dog in Poland that he left with his family. And the dog's name was Schmaltz, due to the color similarity with the chicken fat used in Jewish cooking. Not even a religious person, graduated in the studies of the *Torah* and the *Talmud*, could ignore the fact that it was a legitimate supernatural message. Besides, rumors about the annihilation of the Polish Jews were already around.

After the war, when all the truth came to surface, Rabbi Meyer went back to his city, his street, his house… The place was inhabited by unknown people, but, next door, he found Schmaltz, who recognized him. For a few minutes, he held the dog tight, and, then he left.

During the period of seven days of mourning, praying for his father's soul, Mendel took Moishele to the synagogue. Now a bit older, the boy was curious and asked Mendel why he was praying every day in the temple, with a group of men. He was informed that a son must pray for his father when he dies. Very clever, Moishele asked him what would happen to people who died and didn't have children, not realizing that he could be hurting Mendel, who frowned, and, looking a little sad, answered that there were people in the synagogue that would do it in exchange for some money. Moishele would never forget this explanation.

Also a practitioner of *Umbanda*, Moishele noticed that at Mendel's *terreiro* there were only men praying, while at his mom's there were many women singing. He also realized nobody smoked cigars or drank *cachaça* in the synagogue. As an observer, he felt good in both environments. Neither Mendel motivated him to follow Judaism nor Vicentina to follow *Umbanda*. The boy only kept them company, as if they were going to the movies or the theater.

Mendel enrolled the boy in a public school. Moishele was already "bilingual," as he spoke Yiddish and Portuguese. Sometimes, at home, he indifferently used both languages. He asked for *broit* instead of bread and *wasser* instead of water. So *broit* and *wasser* ended up being part of Vicentina's vocabulary as well.

At school, Moishele had Religion classes. The Christian Church had great influence in education, and Moishele heard about Jesus for the first time. The Religion teacher was a very pale young lady, who looked like a saint, with a soft voice. Suitably, her name was Angelina, and Moishele enjoyed her classes. But he was afraid when he found out about the existence of sins, lots of sins. *There were so many forbidden things!*

Under penalty, another novelty involved going to hell! Nevertheless, he wasn't afraid of the devil, mentioned frequently by the teacher as an evil figure, always tempting men to sin and lose their souls. He had seen "him" at the *terreiro* his mother attended, painted in red and black, and was already familiar with the "Old Scratch," but that fear didn't afflict him.

He liked the look in Jesus's eyes, its intense brightness, radiating kindness and enlightening the world. The holy image, with his *shoulder-length blonde hair* and arms kindly stretched, was a paternal call, for white and black people, no doubt. Concerning the agonizing crucifixion… well, he couldn't understand why they had done it to such a good person.

There was a Priest with a Spanish accent who regularly stopped by the classes. He was a radical, and spoke in anger; he even said, once, that the Jews had killed Christ. Moishele felt uncomfortable with this statement. In his head, a turmoil of contradictions emerged, and he couldn't find the answers. Mendel was a Jew, and he couldn't believe he had killed Jesus. He decided to ask him about it the minute he stepped home, and so he did:

"Mendel, did you kill Jesus Christ?"

Mendel quickly understood his question. The accusation of being the "Deicide People," the Christ-killers, remained for centuries as an excuse for all types of violence against Abraham's people. Here and there, the accusation still sprouted through angry mouths, as an extinguished species that, suddenly, graced us with its presence. Mendel was moved by the boy's sad face and look of disappointment. Of course, he couldn't answer directly the question which was beyond Moishele's childish understanding, he needed to make use of subterfuges in order to live up to his knowledge:

"Moishele, do I look like someone who had killed a person?" Mendel picked up a toy gun. "I don't even have a gun. You have this one. Did you kill Jesus?"

"No, I didn't!" Moishele replied.

Mendel hugged the boy and they laughed, relieved. He had temporarily overcome the case of Jesus being "assassinated" by the Jews.

After coexisting with Judaism and *Umbanda* at home, the contact with the Christian Christianism at school made Moishele very confused. For the first time, he was being told that there was only one way to salvation, and woe to those who weren't baptized; they would "burn in hell." Moishele shrank back every time he thought about the Spanish Priest, who, during his angry preaching, was always staring at him, as he was aware that the student was the son of a *macumbeira* who worked in the house of a Jewish family.

Moishele didn't hide anything from Mendel, as they kept

a very extroverted relationship. He told him everything about those classes, and that he was afraid of going to hell. He confessed he had sinned, he couldn't look away as he saw a naked woman through the neighbor's window.

"Am I going to hell?" Moishele asked.

Joking, Mendel faked a serious face.

"Of course! Of course you are! And you know what? I'm going as well! When I was a kid, during summer, I used to sneak over the wall to see two sisters undressing next door!" Quickly, the fear disappeared, and, as usual, they ended up laughing and hugging each other.

Mendel thought, as a matter of fairness, that he couldn't withhold Moishele's contact with the Christian religion. He would let the future and freewill determine what was to come. On a Sunday morning, he took Moishele to the church, to attend the 8 o'clock mass. But he was out of words when Moishele quietly asked him if they weren't supposed to wet their hands and face in a basin by the door, as other people were doing.

They took a seat in one of the last rows. From behind, someone touched Mendel's shoulder, and, touching his own head, politely mentioned the "little cap." Embarrassed, Mendel realized he hadn't removed his *kippah*.

Moishele, delighted, admired the rows of saints. He was used to the emptiness of the synagogue, with not much to look at, so he was truly impressed with the colorful statues. He concluded, then, that the synagogue was a little dull, with those men praying while holding a book and wearing a striped cloth on their backs.

While in church, he was really moved by two things: That poor Christ nailed to a cross, bleeding, and a saint, whose name he didn't know, with three arrows in his chest. He became curious: *Why do some people go to the synagogue and others to the church? Why isn't there a Christ nailed to a cross in the synagogue? Why do they play drums and dance in my mom's terreiro?*

Concerning the Jew and the son of the *macumbeira* attending mass together, the repercussion of such sacrilege was unavoidable, mainly among a group of very diligent and devoted women. They felt, or pretended to feel uncomfortable with the presence of those two strange beings, indifferent to the sermon and to the sacraments, who didn't even stood up when requested by the Priest or placed coins in the little bag.

The presence of the two "impure" in the neighborhood church caused a reaction between the devotees. They even made a complaint to the parish Priest, who answered that he wasn't allowed to prohibit the entry of any impure, heretic or sinner, on the contrary, "the Church exists to save their souls."

Anyway, the most cold-hearted wouldn't accept such contamination. *How can we commune at peace with those two holding hands, as father and son, and observing the altar as if they were at a concert?* A few days later, all that resulted in a conflict at the street fair. Two of these devotees ran into Vicentina, next to a vegetable stall:

"Are you the one who works at the Jew's house?"

Vicentina frowned:

"I'm Mister Mendel's maid, yes."

"You are a *macumbeira*, aren't you?"

"It's none of your business."

The devotees insisted, shooting:

"You must baptize that boy, leave the *macumba*. What was the Jew doing in the mass with your boy?"

"I agree with whatever Mister Mendel does."

"Don't you know what can happen to a child who isn't baptized?"

"No, I don't, and I couldn't care less."

"He won't get rid of the 'original sin' and he won't go to heaven, his soul will be grieving around."

"Don't worry, he's protected by the orishas."

"And here we go again, talking about that *macumba*, people from the church don't believe in those things."

At this point, Vicentina thought it was better to put an end to the conversation:

"Don't you have some clothes to wash at home?" She turned her back and left, ignoring their words.

The following week, a *despacho*[42] was arranged at the intersection of the street where the devotees lived. It caused great commotion.

"I'm sure it was done by that *macumbeira* working for the Jew!" the two devotees screamed, considering that an investigation wasn't quite necessary to find the obvious person to be blamed and taking into account the *cachaça* bottle, candles, cigars and so on.

The relatives, showing false calmness, took turns checking, through the window, if the "thing" was still there, because the garbage collector should soon be taking it away. But the street cleaner arrived, respectfully looked at "the thing," swept the floor around it and left, taking only the garbage, without touching the *despacho*.

"Take that thing out of here!" the devotees screamed, pointing at the *macumba* and demanding its removal.

The garbage collector pretended he wasn't listening, but due to their insistence he answered with an incisive "No," firmly moving his index finger from side to side. He went his way, leaving the unwelcomed "gift" by the tree. Ignoring the protests and the name-calling, he accelerated his little cart and walked away.

The devotees were in panic. Before going out of the house, they made the sign of the cross and looked away. They asked Priest Felix for help; he took the opportunity to include in his homily a heavy attack against Satan, "who presents himself to men under many guises; it's necessary to know how to recognize the agents of evil, because, many times, they seem to be harmless creatures, and are usually right under your nose."

Proceeding, he implied, not subtly, that the evil was at Mendel's house: "He could be even one of our neighbors, who don't have Jesus in their hearts!" And, to conclude, he announced that, carrying the aspersory and censer, he would

---

42 An *Umbanda* offering.

personally sprinkle Holy Water and incense sacramental steam around the entire street where the devil showed up.

A small group of people walked to the place to be purified. On their way, they passed by Mendel's house, where Vicentina was watering the plants. Anonymous shouts could be heard coming from the group, calling her a *macumbeira*. Vicentina shot them a side-glance. The shouts stopped. Only after the "demon-possessed" got back into the house, the Priest pulled out a huge golden crucifix from under his cassock, and, lifting it very high, he courageously shouted his battle cry:

"Begone, Satan!"

That way, the procession of the Priest and his faithful followers went on, passing through all nearby streets, always under the applause of those who showed up in their windows to give their support to the parochial holy war. Militarily, they passed by the "contaminated" tree, where it was still possible to find parts of the *despacho* placed by the malignant emissary. Even the Priest looked away and pretended he hadn't seen it. But, for security reasons, some meters ahead, he sprinkled a good amount of purified water behind him and vigorously swung the thurible, counting on a providential support from the wind, which was blowing in favor of the sacramental incense.

Mendel knew well those half-dead ghosts of the Inquisition. In his little town, in Poland, sneaking from a half-open window, he observed the processions passing by, and woe betide the Jew who interfered or stopped to see the cortège. During the Holy Week, any Jew who, for a great need, walked on the streets and was seen by the most exalted followers was at risk. There were even some lynchings of the "Christ-killers." Mendel, sometimes, questioned the Lord's "tortuous lines": *Why have You dangerously placed almost all of Your flock in Poland? In a place of anti-Semite predators?*

Christian Poles of a thousand years and Jews shared the same land, two people reciprocally distrustful, two different languages and two incompatible religions. They had two fates violently distinct: the first was subdued; the second, annihilated. That same geographical dilemma, two people in one land, would be extended throughout time and would later, involve the Jews in The Middle East, having a confrontation with the Palestinians.

In the 20th century, poverty was the reason that, providentially, attracted thousands of Hebrews to the Americas, through individual diasporas of salvation. It was like running away from a volcano — the Nazis — that would soon expel its burning lava.

For many, including Mendel, starting a new life in a new place had literally saved their lives. Almost three million people, however, innocently stayed there.

Mendel didn't worry about Moishele's religious future. *Would he be Jew*, Umbandista, *Christian?* He was an enlightened, he neither would impose his religion nor prevent Moishele's access to any other, but he used to offer him guidance concerning the common principles behind several beliefs that, under different names, designated the same deity. At home, as he was fully integrated, Moishele indirectly took part in the prayers and domestic liturgies, such as the Sabbath. Under the same roof, in a separated room, he has accompanied, since he was a baby, his mother's African chants and inhaled incense. Later, already used to the Catechesis at school, Moishele started enjoying the evangelical stories, and was very impressed with the resurrection of Lazarus, the turning of water into wine, the multiplication of the loaves and, above all, the walking on the waters. He felt captivated and involved when he heard "Let the little children come to Me."

In Brazil, during the first half of the 20th century, Christianism was basically an official religion, and, why not say, social as well. From a practical point of view, Mendel thought: *Being a Christian is the "best deal" for Moishele, meaning less discrimination and persecution.* As he didn't consider himself the possessor of the truth, he didn't discourage the boy's contact with Christianity. And he also thought: *The most important, for now, is to lay my cards on the table, "not feather my own nest."*

At that time, people felt embarrassed about assuming a

faith other than the Christian, and Mendel was worried about that. Bureaucratic forms included the item "religion," a way of excluding the non-Christians from the good positions. Also, considering practical reasons, almost every applicant at that time was, or declared to be Christian.

Certainly influenced by the Religion classes, Moishele wanted to pray before sleeping. He asked Mendel to teach him, because he really enjoyed listening to the Lord's Prayer at school and also the Jewish prayers that he has known by heart, since he was very little: *Baruch Atah Adonai...* In that case, as well, Mendel didn't favor any creed in the caption of the boy's soul. He prepared him a special prayer, somewhat truncated, a mixed sequence of his three influences. At bedtime, on his knees, Moishele used to say: "*Baruch Atah Adonai...* Our Father, who art in Heaven, orishas from the Sea and the Earth..."

Mendel was giving it some time. Once a grown up, and able to evaluate life, Moishele would chose a religion. Or not. Although involved in three different religions, officially Moishele was neither a Jew, nor a Christian or an *Umbandista*. He was only a "listener" of the three, even though he has started to distinguish more accurately the visible signs during the services. He attentively observed the white clothes in the *terreiros*, the Priest's long and sparkling outfit while celebrating the mass, the wide, striped cloth that covered the back of the Jews, the lack of purification rituals and Holy Water in the synagogues, the "little cookie" they swallowed from the Priest's hand.

He was puzzled by the Seventh-Day Requiem Mass for the dead, in some cases also on the 30th day or a year after the death, or burial. He thought it was too little to "give" for a loved one, because, in the synagogue, he had witnessed the prayers for the dead practiced daily during eleven months, besides the seven-day mourning, with some people praying up to three times a day in that period. *Was the Christian mass that strong, as it counted on only one or two to solve the future of the deceased? Why did the Jews need such a large number of "masses"? Or was it that, perhaps, they have more sins?*

The Christians would go to either heaven or hell, sometimes passing through a place called "the purgatory". The Jews
should wait for the end of the world to be judged on the Judg-
ment Day, when they would find out their fate. He noticed, as
well, that there were lots of homeless people begging by the
doors of the churches, but not at the synagogue. *Perhaps there
were no poor Jews?* Another thing he considered embarrassing
was that the main figure of the Christians was Jesus Christ, a
Jew. But they also had many other saints. The Jews only prayed
to God, they didn't have saints or orishas.

The event Moishele enjoyed the most about Judaism
used to happen every week, at home: The Sabbath dinner. He
has been fascinated by the brightness of the candles since he
was a little baby, Mrs. Faiga's face covered with a veil, her hands
moving around the silver candlesticks; and, above all, the food,
that she insisted on preparing herself.

He kept weighing up the advantages of each religion:
The Christians had heaven, being enough not to sin much; but
they needed to wait for death before going there. The Jews had
the Sabbath here, every week. The Jews had a day per year in
which they couldn't eat anything; the Christians didn't eat meat
on Friday, when they only ate fish. The Christian Easter was
much better: While the Jews were eating eggs and bitter vege-
tables, the Christians were eating chocolate eggs. Alas, all this
"allowed, not allowed" made him confused, because Mendel,
himself, used to bring him huge Easter eggs; and on Christmas,
a holiday that celebrates the birth of Christ, he used to give him
lots of gifts.

All this thinking about the subtleties and peculiarities of
each devotion indicated that Mendel was reaching his goal, giving Moishele the opportunity to gradually acquire knowledge
of each religion and letting the wisdom of time determine his
option. Empirically, he was conducting him to be a freethinker.

Frequently, the religion of each individual is a "set menu",
passing from parents to children, from children to grandchil-
dren and so on... The baptism, in any form, is a compulsory

"conversion" of someone who will still take a long time until he or she is capable of thinking by him or herself. Once baptized, or something like that, she/ he will automatically follow the steps of his/ her religious movement — communion, *bar mitzvah*, weddings in church or synagogues and respective funerals —, and whoever escapes the pre-established line deserves being called "the lost sheep." Moishele was a rare case. Mendel allowed him to be free from any religious imposition.

Faiga, with her permanent existential trauma, remained neutral; she wasn't able to have a say in Vicentina's son's life. She was a thin woman, red-haired, fairly beautiful, with some freckles on her face. When she arrived in Brazil with Mendel, they were not in love, but already in need of each other, as they were facing the great unknown after a thirty-day on board apprehension.

Faiga left Poland engaged, by arrangement, to a cousin she only knew through pictures, who was waiting for her on the other side of the Atlantic. When they disembarked, there was the "fiancé," Leon, carrying a huge sunflower bouquet. They recognized each other, but poor Prince Charming, who became very excited after seeing his bride, almost burst into tears when she told him the epistolary commitment had been broken. She told him how grateful she had been, but informed him that she had met and became fond of another man. She comforted him, saying he was good-looking, and would soon find another fiancée...

Getting over the shock, Leon addressed the practical side of the question:

"What about the travel expenses? The ticket, the papers?"

"I insist on paying all expenses," Mendel intervened.

Frustrated, but refunded, the ex-fiancé, crestfallen, left the wharf of Praça Mauá taking back the sunflowers, which he didn't throw away.

After the war, hearing about the annihilation of her family, poor Faiga was deeply depressed. She sought total protection in Mendel, her guide to the outside world, meaning whatever was beyond the gate of their house. Moishele's presence still hurt, stealing her husband's attention, but she didn't interfere in their relationship. She wasn't hostile to the boy, only indifferent. It took her some time to become fond of him, something that would casually happen.

A big circus arrived in town. Mendel saw the ad of the show, and remembered that the only circus he had seen was in Poland, from the outside, as he didn't have money for the ticket; he tried to get in with other boys, through the tarp; but he didn't make it, because he was caught by a guard. Then there was another circus, and he could afford it either.

He had cried a lot, and was still crying. *Would it be a betrayal of the ones murdered by gas to be in such a place?* The cruel, not witnessed memories, tended to accommodate in the relationship with those who suddenly found their families reduced to yellowish pictures brought in suitcases. This defensive nature of the memory allowed them to go to a place where people would laugh and have fun — tricks of the human mind.

Mendel managed to overcome the pain and guilt. The curiosity, accumulated over decades, made him excited; he had no idea of what a circus looked like from the inside, he had never seen a clown — his biggest wish. He had a hard time making a decision, it wasn't fair thinking only of himself; imagining Moishele's laughter, his conscious mingled his own desire with a sort of paternal obligation. Faiga didn't oppose; always apathetic and indifferent to everything, she accompanied her husband.

Sitting in the bleacher, under a green tarp roof, Mendel, Moishele and Faiga couldn't resist the show; it was the same as seeing the ocean for the first time. It took Faiga some time to enjoy it, but she threw in the towel when the clown kicked his partner's butt — he had Hitler's hair and mustache.

While leaving, stepping on the floor covered with sawdust, before coming back to "real" life, Moishele, provided with happiness, led by Mendel's hand, stretched his other hand and held Faiga's, who fondly squeezed it. From then on, Moishele had two mothers.

Over fifty years old, Faiga felt, for the first time, a bit of borrowed maternity, the fleeting "mother" of a boy who has been living in her house for quite a while. The Jew Faiga was, finally, the latecomer *Yiddish mama* of a seven-year old black boy, in agreement with the biological mother, who accepted, without jealousy, her mistress' new behavior.

Faiga's "awakening" brought up an increased, latent instinct, which ruled for centuries the Jewish maternal-filial relationship. The first change in her behavior, of course, involved food: She started stuffing Moishele, and was baking a cake after the other. The minute he showed up, she would come with something to eat, and she insisted that leftover food wasn't allowed. She thought he was too thin. For that reason, aside from cakes, she closely supervised all his meals.

"Eat it up, eat it up!" she repeated, with a sort of fanaticism.

Diplomatic, recognizing Faiga as a new, much healthier person, Mendel tried to balance his wife's obsession, preventing the boy from gaining too much weight.

Faiga was also concerned about Moishele's school development. She checked his grade report, the notebooks, and inspected his homework. She was already dreaming of her "son's" brilliant future; he would probably be a doctor, or an engineer, the primary wish of Jewish mothers, *why not?* With the idea of coming closer to him, she bought Yiddish books and started teaching him the idiom. Already familiar with Mendel's and Faiga's daily language, Moishele was doubly alphabetized, and his polyglot condition would be proven useful in many future situations.

In one of them, he saved Mendel from a great financial loss. One evening, two brothers, very important businessmen of the Jewish community, came to Mendel's house. Delighted with such distinguished presences — *Saul and Samuel Epstein in my house... Who could imagine it?* —, Mendel quickly offered them his best liquor, and asked Faiga to bring some cookies.

"What can they possibly want?" Faiga whispered, suspicious.

"Whatever it is, coming from these people, it can't be bad!" Mendel answered.

In fact, there were reasons for such excitement. Saul and Samuel Epstein were prominent figures among the most important institutions, key-reference among the local Jews. In the commercial environment, they were synonyms of correction and financial growth. Only being physically close to them would make one proud.

"To what do I owe the honor of your visit?" Mendel asked, smiling.

Saul went straight to the point:

"We're buying a big piece of land in the South zone.[43] We'll build a hotel, the biggest ever built in Rio de Janeiro. We've got, basically, all the money we need to close the deal, I said basically, because we found out that we still miss a small amount, ten percent of the total value."

Samuel kept talking:

"So, we thought: Why not selecting some respected patricians instead of asking the banks? We know that the Caixa Econômica[44] pays *drek*[45] interests. As we are people known for being serious and everybody trusts our way of conducting businesses, we are accepting loans, for only sixty days. Nobody doubts it, as we're talking about doing business with Saul and Samuel; we'll pay slightly higher interests, as it is an absolutely reliable *guesheft*,[46] we'll pay the promissory notes on the exact due date, not a day after."

Mendel couldn't stop showing his gratitude. He felt proud they thought of him, and insisted on giving them a good amount of money he had at home. The following day, he would withdraw the money he had deposited in Caixa Econômica.

Saul and Samuel in my house... he repeated to himself proudly, while walking to the room where he kept a safety box.

---

43 A fancy neighborhood in Rio, where Copacabana is located.
44 Brazilian bank, controlled by the Brazilian government.
45 "Shit" in Yiddish.
46 Business in Yiddish.

Meanwhile, completely ignoring the young black boy in a corner of the room, fixing a lampshade — *a servant, for sure* —, the big shots, speaking Yiddish in a relaxed matter, recapped, feeling really proud, the several loans they had already got, mocking the good faith of those who had believed them.

"We already got more money than we planned!" Saul said.

"No wonder!" Samuel mocked. "With your sweet-talk and our respected commercial past, they would beg to lend us the money."

"In less than a week, those who have kissed our hands will curse us, and our following generations. Men above suspicious becoming the kings of swindle!" Saul cynically added.

"By this time our ears will be far away from all the swearing; first Buenos Aires, then Europe, and, finally, Israel, where all 'our capital' will be," Samuel said, ironically.

"If we think about it, we're not cheating anyone. We asked for money to build a hotel, and that's what we'll do. The point is that we will not do it in Copacabana, but in Tel Aviv, a simple geographical detail," Saul replied, laughing.

Samuel also couldn't help laughing. Moishele finished fixing the lampshade and, "invisible" for both of them, who completely ignored his presence, went straight to Mendel's room, where, with the safety box opened, he was counting the money.

"Mendel, I need to tell you something," Moishele said.

"Yeah, yeah," Mendel answered, still counting the money.

"Those two men are crooks."

"Crooks? Who are you talking about?"

"Those two in the living room."

"Saul and Samuel?"

"I don't know their names, all I know is that they're crooks, and they are staging a coup to keep your money."

"Are you nuts, Moishele? Saul and Samuel Epstein are the most respected men in our community. They are great businessmen, and have always honored their deals. My money is saved with them as much as it's saved in my box. How could you come up with such story? Forget it, you're completely wrong."

Faiga, who was listening to the conversation from a distance, intervened:

"Let Moishele speak, Mendel."

"All right. Talk, Moishele. Why are you making such serious accusation against these honored people?"

The young boy told him all the conversation he had just heard.

"Did you understand all that in Yiddish?" Mendel was astonished, surprised with the boy's fluency in the language.

He was convinced. Saved, at the last minute, from a financial disaster, Mendel hugged him and more than ever considered him his son. Faiga proudly joined them, and they celebrated that brief family moment.

Mendel still had to disengage himself from those two crooks, who already considered it a quick win, and kept on taking advantage of people's good faith through their scams, two men whom, until then, he unconditionally admired and considered as confident investors. Mendel went back to the living room, hiding his deception:

"My dear friends, unfortunately, it won't be today that I'll have the honor to be an associate of such important enterprise. Forgive me, but my wife deposited yesterday in Caixa Econômica the money I was keeping at home. There was a burglary nearby and she thought it was better not to keep that much money. But, tomorrow morning, I'll withdraw the money and take it to your office."

"Do it as soon as possible, because we'll be very busy talking to our patricians, who keep coming to us for investing, including Rabbi Meyer, who had already given us part of his money and, tomorrow, will bring a bit more," Samuel said.

"I'm not surprised; people know that they won't find a better place to invest than with Saul e Samuel Epstein. Tomorrow, I'll be there, early, no excuse!" the "almost" victim theatrically added. They said goodbye with mutual hypocrisy.

"*Shalom!*"
"*Shalom!*"

Mendel didn't even dare to talk to his friends about Saul and Samuel and their financial investments, as his suspicion would be considered heresy: "You are *meshuggah*, Mendel, what's happening to you? How can anyone, mainly a Jew, imagine such an absurd? We believe in them more than we believe in *Banco do Brasil*,"[47] they would say. He didn't go to their office as agreed. They called many times, but he didn't talk to them, Faiga came up with several excuses. He resisted the telephone harassment, but, in some moments, he doubted Moishele's version.

He probably wouldn't be able to resist longer, perhaps two or three days. At the height of his doubt, however, passing by Praça Onze, he noticed a hustle and bustle; many groups were expressing a feeling of revolt because of something that had happened. He got closer and realized that the reason of the collective fury was the pair: Saul and Samuel Epstein had run away with the money from a large part of the Jewish community, not even the Rabbi was left out. Only the ones who didn't have money were saved. Nobody knew where they had run to, the speculation was: The United States or Israel?

The revolt was even more painful because the victims of the two financial executioners, for many reasons, couldn't talk or complain about it. First, because the promissory notes were, then, just pieces of paper, with no power to catch the debtors. Second, because if somehow any information about the coup reached the press, it would feed the fire concerning anti-Semitism, not to mention that the Tax Authorities would probably question the origin of that amount of money. At times like these, vanity and arrogance work the other way around. Some who had suffered loses didn't mention the real value of the amount lost, falsely trying to soften the blow and saying that "very little" was taken, and stating that Levy, Ytzek and Natan had lost much more.

---

47 Brazilian bank, controlled by the Brazilian government.

Mendel walked away from that "Western Wall." He felt relieved, but scared, as someone who had just escaped from some sort of serious accident. He tried to learn a lesson from the incident: *On the subject of money, I'll never trust anyone again, the ones who look honest are the most dangerous; life is full of traps, we are doing well in a minute and, suddenly, you can hit bottom, such as those desperate men at Praça Onze. Who would say Saul and Samuel, honored members of the community, were refined crooks? To fool your own brothers...*

He recapitulated the facts since the day he saw that baby under the rain in his mother's arms, how he covered them with his umbrella and invited them in. If he had arrived a minute earlier, he wouldn't have found them, his son Moishele wouldn't have entered his life and he would have been ruined. Concerning the money kept at home, actually much more than the necessary, he questioned himself if he had somehow broken any Talmudic precept. He thought: *As much as time goes by, we forget that money is a mean, not an end; this must be written in some part of the* Talmud, *and if it isn't, it should well be.*

While driving home, mulling over the incident, he remembered that since his arrival in Brazil he had never taken a long trip; in order to save money, he had never left the country. As he was now rich, it was the time to travel without regard to costs. He thought mainly about those unfortunate men who had lost so much money to those crooks. *How many times have they deprived themselves of many things to save that amount of money that was now vanished?*

He talked to Faiga and Moishele about his idea. Faiga, at the beginning, got excited, imagining they would go to nearby cities, but, in contrast to Moishele, she held back when Mendel told them he would like to travel to Europe and Israel. Faiga, then, confessed her unbeatable fear of flying, she wouldn't be able to accompany her husband this time. She suggested they should go together, Mendel and Moishele. Vicentina supported the idea, and all was set: they would travel in three months, in July, during the school vacation.

5. THE JOURNEY

Mendel was born in Ostrow, a tiny city in Poland. London, Paris and Rome were, still, only names, inaccessible as the moon. Moishele, anxious, checked all the main tourist attractions in advance, through all the literature he could find. They would start their journey in Italy.

Vicentina was truly proud. She never thought of her son on an airplane, flying over the world. She would ask the orishas to protect them, and Mendel thanked her:

"Great! Next to him on the same plane, I'll be protected as well."

On board, the long plane trip led to an exciting talk about the Old World. Moishele's curiosity about the European continent made Mendel feel, simultaneously, excited and uncomfortable concerning the young man's geographic questions. Yes, he, Mendel, was European, but, due to life circumstances, he didn't know anything about the other countries, as he left Ostrow to emigrate. He slipped out of Moishele's questions, as any father who doesn't want to feel embarrassed in front of his kid. When asked, he went off on a tangent:

"Calm down, boy, don't ruin the surprise. Very soon, we'll be there and you will be able to see it by yourself."

He thought it was strange that Moishele was insistently asking about the Vatican. Although familiar with Vicentina's *Umbanda*, and also involved with Mendel's Judaism, he was really excited about seeing the Holy See.[48] And it was not only to buy a souvenir or some religious object to Vicentina, who used to say she had never liked priests.

Luckily, they arrived in the Italian capital on a Sunday, the day Pope Pius XII used to come to the window to give his blessing *urbi et orbi*.[49] Into the crowd, they finally saw the Sovereign Pontiff waving. The first obligation while in Rome, religious or touristic, has been accomplished.

They also visited the Saint Peter's Basilica. Respectfully, Mendel didn't forget to take off his *kippah* as soon as they set foot in the impressive nave. Moishele, astounded, couldn't help comparing such grandiosity to the small synagogue and the *terreiro* he attended. Having a touch of Christianism, due to his religion classes at school, he asked Mendel if he could pray.

"Of course! After all, the person who started all this was that Jew there, crucified!" Mendel pointed, playful, but quite vain.

Due to lack of habit, Moishele didn't know by heart any complete Christian prayer, but, pushing his memory, he was able to say the Lord's Prayer missing only a few words. The teenager was very impressed with the visits to the Basilica in Vatican and the Sistine Chapel; he was stunned by such magnificence and beauty, he was moved by the superb artwork made by human hands. As he visited humble *terreiros*, small synagogues and few district churches, he couldn't possibly believe that something like that could have been built in the name of a religion. Seeing wonders such as the "Pietá,"[50] in Saint Peter's Cathedral, stretched neck pointing to the sky, mesmerized by Michelangelo's frescoes on the ceiling and walls of the chapel, he wondered if he really wanted to be part of that.

---

48 The universal government of the Catholic Church that operates from Vatican City State.
49 Latin, mening "to the city (Rome) and to the world."
50 A masterpiece of Renaissance sculptured by Michelangelo, housed in St. Peter's Basilica in Vatican.

Would that be the true religion? So powerful... He knew he would see nothing like that, God stretching his hand to the first man of the Creation. Moishele was interested in aesthetics, he had already been impressed by the pictures of the Christian churches he saw in books and magazines, mainly the Gothic, with its arches supported by pilasters rising up to the sky — they were like indicative arrows of supernatural inspiration. He asked Mendel if the Jews had temples that big. Mendel didn't miss the chance and was a bit ironic, jealous of Moishele's enchantment concerning the cathedrals.

"At the moment, we don't. We used to have two really big ones, but 'they' came and destroyed everything."

"When was that?"

"Over two thousand years ago, in Jerusalem."

"And the Jews? Did they remain without a place to pray?"

"Well... we used a great wall that was left, but there we can only pray standing."

"Who destroyed the temples?"

"Nebuchadnezzar was one of them; he destroyed the First Temple and took us — Mendel regarded this as personal matter — as slaves to Babylon. Six centuries after, the Romans came, destroyed our Second Temple and spread us throughout Europe. As the world turns, I ended up in Grajaú."

"So, when it was raining, didn't the Jews have a place to pray? Only inside their houses?"

"There was a time we couldn't pray even in our houses! Whomever said our prayers would be burned in bonfires by the fanatics of the Inquisition."

"Does this history ever come to an end? What have we done?"

Mendel was moved by the "we", coming out of Moishele's mouth.

"When you arrived home, in your mother's arms, in 1938, for example, the Germans were burning hundreds of synagogues in Germany."

"What a loss, uh, Mendel?"

Mendel followed the same line:

"That's why, until today, no one wants to insure synagogues."

The young boy wouldn't accept all those persecutions motivated by religion. He argued, showing precocious ecumenism:

"Mendel, I can't understand all that suffering related to religion; wouldn't it be enough to accept the strongest religion in each moment of danger? Why insist? Don't you think it's stubbornness? Take me, for example; according to the occasion I'm *Umbandista*, then Christian, then Jew... Only the prayers change, but it's always about praise and request."

Surprised, Mendel thought a little. And agreed:

"You're right, but what can I do? We Jews are very stubborn."

After visiting the biggest religious constructions, the postcards of the European Christendom such as the Vatican, The Milan Cathedral, Notre-Dame and the Westminster Abbey, Moishele regretted the lack of, at least, one synagogue big enough to be a touristic reference. They had seen some, but they were very simple. He realized Europe was an entirely Christian territory, not so suitable for the Jews.

In Israel, for sure, he would be able to find such architectural greatness. In two thousand years, they would have had enough time to build another big temple, Moishele believed, unfamiliar with the historical and political circumstances.

When Mendel, while in Israel, told him they were going to visit the most sacred place of Judaism, Moishele immediately thought about some kind of monumental construction, perhaps not comparable to the Vatican or the Notre-Dame Cathedral, but something grand, the sun on Earth for the children of Abraham.

"There it is!" Mendel exclaimed, sparkling eyes, tears rolling, heart beating fast. He was pointing at a distant wall made of stone, where a few faithful were praying, wearing their black overcoats and hats.

Mendel was confused about their presence in that place, which, at the time, belonged to the Arabs. For sure, they had paid good money for a tourism agency in order to have access to the wall. He and Moishele weren't allowed closer.

From far away, in contrast to the clarity of the wall, the orthodox looked like notes on a sheet music. Holding a book in their hands, they prayed, shuckling close to the stones.

"Interesting," Moishele commented. "But where is the big sacred place?"

"You are looking at it!" Mendel answered.

"All I can see is a huge stone wall. How can you compete with the great Saint Peter's Basilica with that?"

"It's not 'any' wall, it's part of the wall which protected the Temple, this is what's left, I already told you. The Romans destroyed it two thousand years ago, and, not yet satisfied, they spread the Jews around the world, that's why it's called The Western (Wailing) Wall, we cry for the loss and destruction of the Temple that used to be here. It's a pity they won't let us get there, it's under Arab domination. One day, who knows..."

"And why don't you build another temple, such as the Vatican? Jews around the world could chip in."

Mendel couldn't help laughing about his suggestion. *All the Jews around the world "chipping in" for the construction of a new Temple...*

"That's it, I like the idea. Let's meet prime minister David Ben-Gurion[51] today and I'll tell him that: 'Minister, my son proposes that Jews from all over the world chip in for the construction of a big Temple.' "

Moishele accepted Mendel's irony, and gave him a tit-for-tat answer:

"But you have to mention that they have to chip in *kosher*[52] money."

---

51 The primary founder and the first prime minister of Israel.
52 The word *kosher* can be used with the idea of something being legitimate, permissible. The opposite is also used, "non-*kosher.*"

Mendel, then, laughed out loud. Thinking and calculating, Moishele commented:

"If the Second Temple was destroyed in the year 70 A.D., so it was here that He expelled the 'peddlers' when he was 30 years or so..."

The Religion classes left their impact.

Mendel, not demonstrating, was a bit bothered by his observation, right there, physically next to the ancient scenery described in the New Testament; after all, such "peddlers" would be Jews, as himself, his ancestors, not followers of Jesus. But, for the sake of consistency, he agreed. He chose not to go deep into the subject and didn't contest; long ago, he had decided to leave Moishele free from any religious imposition. Influenced by what he remembered from his religion classes, the boy invited Mendel to go to the Holy Sepulcher and the Via Dolorosa, also known as The Way of the Cross.

"Via Dolorosa?" Mendel asked, puzzled.

It was time for Moishele to take on the role of a teacher:

"It's the way Jesus had to walk carrying his cross until the Golgotha."

"Golgotha?" Mendel, again, demonstrated he was unaware of anything out of the Old Testament.

"It's the place where they crucified Jesus, the Mount Calvary."

Mendel was impressed with Moishele's facility to talk about parts of the New Testament. But he didn't consider it as any kind of tendency. Actually, Mendel, himself, felt a frisson while walking through the several Stations, stoppages of Jesus while walking to the place of the crucifixion — a short distance separated the most sacred place of Judaism, the *Kotel*,[53] from the most sacred place of Christendom.

Being here doesn't mean I'm offending my faith, I'm a tourist as any other, he thought to himself. But Moishele's excitement, impacted by the Via Dolorosa and the Holy Sepul-

---

53 Hebrew, meaning "wall."

cher, caught his eyes. Mendel, naturally, started regarding the possibility of the boy's conversion to Christianism. Perhaps it was time to be officially bound up with a religion.

Mendel was wrong. Moishele felt good concerning the quietness of the Christian masses and the Jewish services, but he also enjoyed the *terreiro*, with all the dancing and African drums. He was attracted to all religions. In each one, he could find something that touched his spirit. In the *Umbanda*, for example, he could find the primitive simplicity of the liturgies, the chants, the food, the incorporation of spirits, the orishas of the nature. The syncretism, instrument of survival of the African faith, was somewhat similar to the new Christians at the time of the Inquisition, when the converted Jews lived under a severe inspection, bordering on the ridiculous; externally, they worshiped the Christian saints, but in their hearts remained followers of the Mosaic Law, and secretly practiced it. During an inspection trip in Brazil, the inquisitors even placed public notes in churches encouraging the population to report people who didn't eat pork or work on Saturdays.

To counterbalance Jerusalem's Christian impact on Moishele, Mendel arranged a visit to Masada, an ancient mountaintop fortress where the Jews heroically resisted the Romans between 66 and 73 A.D. It was clear that visiting a place where a long battle had taken place, and all rebels had killed themselves, affected the boy's mind. It was, however, an emotion originated from History, not something biblical, linked to a spiritual message of the Holy Land. Moishele proudly compared the battle in Masada to the resistance of fugitive slaves in the Palmares Quilombo.[54]

Mendel carefully listened to him and agreed. Then, Moishele asked Mendel to take him to any place Moses, the liberator of the People of Israel, had been. A bit choked, Mendel answered that such places didn't exist, since Moses hadn't entered the Promised Land and had just seen it from afar.

---

54 A maroon settlement in Brazil, in the 17th century.

"Why? Did he die before arriving?"

"No! He was punished because, once, he doubted the Lord's words. But before that he received the Tables of the Law, with the Ten Commandments."

Moishele was sad to hear that Moses — his "namesake" by nickname — hadn't arrived there, the land in which he was stepping on. He compared the fates of the two men sent from God: Jesus was condemned for entering Jerusalem and preaching his doctrine; Moses couldn't even enter into Canaan, the place that, in the future, would be Jerusalem.

"Religion is not an easy topic," he commented.

"You're right. That's why we count on faith," Mendel replied.

Frustrated, feeling sorry for the main figure of Judaism, Moishele had to settle for a miniature of Moses' sculpture[55] made in plaster, which he bought as a souvenir. But he was still confused:

"Why can't we find statues of Moses in Israel? Actually, of any prophet? Even in the countryside of Minas Gerais,[56] in the city of Congonhas, we have the Twelve Prophets of the Scriptures by *Aleijadinho*...[57] I think it would be fair to have a statue of Moses in Mount Sinai, as we have Christ the Redeemer in Rio de Janeiro."

He didn't get an answer.

However, the most surprising situation wasn't related to places or sacred symbols. It happened at their hotel reception. While Mendel was checking out, he was informed, by the manager, that his bill had already been paid.

"There must be a mistake, I haven't paid anything yet!" Mendel said.

"This is what I was told, Mister," the manager answered.

"Who told you that?" Mendel asked.

"The owner of the hotel," the man confirmed.

---

55 By Michelangelo.
56 A State in the Southeastern region of Brazil.
57 18th century Brazilian sculptor and architect.

Mendel was confused. He was sure it was all a great mistake. Why would the owner of the hotel offer him such courtesy? He wasn't an important person, neither a politician nor a well-known artist.

"Have you checked my name? Are you sure about that? My name is Mendel Rosenstrauch."

"No doubts, Mister, that's what I was told by Mister Saul."

"Who is Mister Saul?"

"Saul Epstein, the owner of this hotel, he met you in Brazil. By chance, he was walking nearby and saw when you arrived; then he told me not to charge anything from his Brazilian friend."

Mendel and Moishele exchanged glances, while they were having a look at the magnificent entrance hall. Yes, there it was, luxuriously materialized, through beautiful stones, thick rugs and rich furniture, part of the money taken from the unwary Isaacs, Jacobs and Abrahams in Rio de Janeiro.

Mendel was quietly waiting for Moishele's reaction. *Would he accept the generosity of a crook? The result of something dishonest, non-kosher?* Mendel thought for a few seconds, and bluntly answered:

"Tell Mister Epstein that we are grateful."

"You can say it yourself, Mister, he's coming this way," the receptionist pointed, using his chin, to Saul, who was coming forward, smiling.

Mendel didn't have time to think about a different attitude and accepted the hug from the old crook, who was absolutely calm, scattering prosperity. Saul noticed Mendel's hesitation, and was frank and straight to the point:

"Mendel, let's not pretend nothing happened. We two know quite well what happened. I'm not proud of it, but it's done. Here, I try not to think about it. Concerning my creditors, rightly or wrongly, I see them as non-voluntary collaborators of the pioneer Zionist cause. This hotel was practically bankrupt when I bought it, I completely remodeled it and changed its name!"

Facing such shameless cynicism, Mendel didn't want to be aggressive, although it would be very suitable. He chose to change the subject and started talking about the wonders he had been visiting in the young State of Israel. He didn't spare compliments to the hotel, which was called, through premeditated coincidence and exacerbated egocentricity, "King Saul Hotel."

Saul looked at them, curious:

"Who is this *schwarze*?[58] What's he doing here with you?"

"He's my son," Mendel said, surprising his interlocutor, who had never considered such possibility.

After the usual trivialities of moments like that, when old friends meet, mainly when one of them emigrated and is dying of curiosity to know what people are talking about him back home, Mendel, requested by Saul, reproduced in Yiddish and Portuguese all the bad names the fugitive brothers were being called in Brazil.

Updated, but not surprised, Saul couldn't control his curiosity. As everything was openly unmasked, and he was on safe ground, he wanted to know how Mendel "had escaped" him.

"Ask him," Mendel answered, turning to his son.

Perplexed, Saul listened to Moishele, who told him in Yiddish, with the finest details, the conversation between the brothers who stopped by Mendel's house that night, including the escape plan to take the investors' money. They had loosened their tongues, and comfortably talked about the planned coup, thinking they were "alone" while the "victim" had left to take the money from the safety box. Quickly, Saul remembered the black little boy who was fixing the lampshade. They didn't worry about his presence; after all, they thought they were speaking a language that he wouldn't be able to understand. Saul couldn't believe it.

"How could I imagine the black boy would speak our idiom as a young boy from the ghetto?"

Sarcastically, Mendel asked Saul:

58 Derogatory Yiddish slang for a black person.

"Would you like me to take any message to your friends, your creditors in Brazil?"

Saul was even more sarcastic, and answered:

"Tell them that the money they had put in my hands allowed the *aliyah*,[59] since they had chosen to be away from the homeland of their ancestors, calmly working in their businesses in Rio de Janeiro."

They were trading barbs, no hard feelings, because Mendel escaped Saul's "patriotic" endeavor unharmed.

Mendel concluded, with typical Jewish irony:

"If another pioneer investor, such as yourself, shows up there, those who aren't broken yet..."

Saul smiled before he could finish the sentence, and, suddenly, he bowed his head, looking serious, thoughtful. Mendel could see a hint of regret. Before saying goodbye, as a formality, he asked about Saul's brother and partner.

"How about Samuel? How is he?"

Saul would rather not listen to this question. But he answered, looking sad:

"Samuel passed away."

Mendel didn't disrespect the memory of the deceased. He wanted to know what happened.

"Died of what? He was relatively young..."

"High blood pressure!"

Mendel thought it was strange.

"High blood pressure? But here, in Israel, there are great doctors and public hospitals, wasn't him taking care of himself?"

Saul felt embarrassed about explaining the facts. He didn't want any merciless person, cognizant of Samuel's history, to interpret what happened as a punishment. With a forced abandon, he tried to complete the information.

"Actually, he drowned in the Dead Sea."

Again, Mendel couldn't help being surprised:

"Drowned in the Dead Sea? It's impossible, nobody can

---

59 Hebrew word meaning "ascent" or "go up," referring to the *return* to the *Promised Land.*

drown there! The water is so salty that people float, even if they try hard to sink."

Saul, finding no way out, realized he had to continue and explain how everything had really happened, even knowing that many people would "enjoy" the fact and its circumstances. Almost crying, he continued:

"He didn't really drown... due to the hot weather, he briefly fainted while bathing, and drank that water, which is pure salt. This has caused a serious hypertension crisis, which killed him!"

He asked Mendel, even knowing it was useless, not to mention the story to anyone in Brazil. Mendel, also knowing it was useless saying, ensured that he wouldn't utter a word about Samuel's death. He was maliciously subtle:

"It's water under the bridge... All I can do is to express my sincere condolences on the loss of your brother, and, at the same time, say *Mazal Tov*."

Saul didn't understand. Mendel explained:

"Condolences on the loss of a partner and brother; and congratulations for doubling your fortune, as you were his only heir. As far as I know, Samuel didn't have other living relatives."

They said goodbye through an almost sincere hug. In the cab, going to the airport, Mendel's foretaste "escaped":

"Ah, when people hear this story at Praça Onze..."

Moishele, surprised to detect Mendel's unprecedented sadism, gave him an odd look.

6. POLAND

The last part of the trip had started, and this time it was not about tourism or leisure, on the contrary, it would be tense and painful. They were going to Poland. Mendel wanted to revisit his hometown, not his family or close relatives, as there was no one left in Ostrow. Going back was an imperative of consciousness, a return to an imaginary time, to a place where he kissed and hugged goodbye so many people — father, mother, uncles, cousins, friends... He didn't know that through all the distress caused by leaving he was escaping the Nazi annihilation. Ahead, "a ship, an ocean and a land full of opportunities," they used to say.

Through the window of the train he had lost sight of them, without knowing it would be forever. In 1942, from that same platform, the ones who had stayed would also leave, but in different train cars, to another direction, taking a trip without laughter, hope or return.

But Mendel was coming back. *For what,* he asked himself, and answered his own question: *You don't go back to a place, you go back to someone... but to whom... if they are no longer there?* However, it was important to go back. If he had decided not to revisit his little town — his improbable home, the streets he had walked, the carp pond, the public Polish school he had attended — he would have kept similar memories to those of ordinary immigrants, who slowly and naturally lost touch with their homeland. They took longer to answer family letters, until it all became simple images in their memories, blurred by time. To go back, feel the buzz, listen to Yiddish everywhere, feel the smells of the weekly market, close his eyes and listen to the sounds of the shoemakers working, touch, one more time, his grandfather's huge silver scissors — he was a tailor —, be attentive to the water seller's call... home voices... the synagogue singer, many, many voices. Voices... they were the most alive memories left.

It was necessary to go back. After tragedies, the ones who stayed normally recover the victim's bodies, but, in Ostrow, not even the bodies were left. It felt as he was going back to bury them in his heart. During World War I, Mendel was there. Still a kid, he witnessed the arrival of the invaders, then friendly Germanic soldiers. But during World War II, already in Brazil, he didn't see the swastika on the armbands of the SS. The memory related to such "kindness" of the German army during World War I was responsible for the fact that many people hadn't become desperate or tried to escape before the imminent arrival of the Nazis in 1939.

In October 1942, the Holocaust train took them to a place called Treblinka.[60] Due to lack of communication during the conflict, the information about the total annihilation arrived three years later. It was a great shock, and he went through a long period of melancholy. Mendel felt the necessity of returning to his homeland to cry.

The physical distance separating them, the time of this separation, the imposed lack of information and his new life in Brazil had provoked an image dissolution in his mind. The individual ends up getting used to absences, of alive and deceased people; concerning the mind, absence is absence, that's why Mendel hadn't cried. It was a "dry" pain, a crying with no tears, as if all of them were still there and his memory was already used to their absence. He wanted to add color to the faded images.

---

60 Major Nazi concentration camp and extermination camp, located near the village of *Treblinka*, 50 miles northeast of Warsaw.

Many non-religious places had "survived" in Ostrow. Walking slowly on the streets he used to play as a kid, and passing by friend's houses, he felt the pain of calling someone without getting an answer. *This*, he thought, *reestablished the connection between the day he left and the moment he returned, as nothing had happened in between, as he had never left them, as all of them would be really gone only at the moment he set foot there again.*

Since 1942, there hasn't been anyone in Ostrow who, running into him, would ask: "What's new, Mendel?" There have been, however, scenes of a dead past that popped up in his memory, even more alive: the picnic on the grass by the river, until the day a *goy* bought the land for farming purposes; the frozen lake, in which, while ice-skating with friends, he sank beneath the broken ice; the bravery of the young girls, facing heavy snow during dawn to get to the brush factory on time; his fear of going out on Holy Friday, due to the risk of being beaten and accused of being a "Christ-killer."

Such memories had survived and kept "stored," because, all of a sudden, a train had arrived and abruptly taken thousands of passengers away, each one with his/ her uncertainties, useless bags and bundles very well identified to avoid being lost or taken at the time of the departure.

Mendel had met some survivors from Ostrow in Israel, people who miraculously had escaped and witnessed everything, even the arrival of the train cars. He had heard from them that, a few days before the invasion of Poland, the city was really tense. All kinds of rumors had been spread, mainly when they started convoking young men to be part of the Army and sending other men to construct shelters and trenches. The Jews tried, then, to capture the transmission of the Polish radio station, and, on September 1st 1939, they heard the Germans had declared war against Poland.

A few days later, Ostrow was full of refugees and German bombs started dropping. Even the few people who had a car had to run away by carts pulled by donkeys, as there was no gasoline. On September 6th, the streets were deserted. People were hiding in the basements. In the afternoon, a German patrol arrived. At night, they burned part of the Jewish businesses. Already established, the German administration falsely stated that Poles and Jews would receive the same treatment, and asked all of them to keep working normally. Then, for a few months, Ostrow lived a period of deceptive security; the policy of extermination hadn't started yet. Some young people, among those telling this history to Mendel, hadn't believed the apparent peace, and had used the opportunity to run away.

At the beginning of 1940, the racial laws entered into force: The Jews living in the city were forced to hand over great amounts of money, gold and silver, close their businesses, stores, factories and shops; all synagogues had their ornaments taken. The Jews couldn't leave town without previous permission; curfew and the use of an identifying yellow Star of David on the clothes were imposed — preliminary steps of the Holocaust in Ostrow.

As Mendel was being informed about the chronology of the extermination, he simultaneously recapitulated his life in Rio. In 1939, when the war started and Poland was invaded, he stopped receiving letters from his family. The Jews in Brazil didn't consider it a problem, after all, it was a "war thing." *How could they harm the Jews without harming the Poles?* Some months after the invasion, the Brazilian newspapers didn't publish anything about any widespread atrocity, except the destruction of Warsaw by the *Luftwaffe*.[61]

Without news, gossips and rumors were popping up. As they were far away and feeling secure, the biggest fear of the families, naively, was related to the possibility of someone being hit by a bomb dropped from a plane. How could they have possibly known this was the smallest of risks? How could they have given wings to the absurd in their imagination? How could they have thought about a hypothetical genocide, as Mendel was

---

61 The German air force before and during World War II.

peacefully walking through Praça Saens Peña with Faiga and Moishele, having ice cream and looking for a good movie? How could they have imagined that, at that right moment, they were already building the first gas chambers and that the "Final Solution"[62] had been set in motion? How could they have known that, after a few months, mother, father, uncles and cousins would have literally vanished?

Without the answers to these questions, how could they have cried for them? They had already been taken to Treblinka never to return, while in Brazil they were living in hope, a characteristic of the Hebrew spirit. The "last train" left Ostrow in October 1942, and, for not being aware of the facts, the *Kaddish* for the ones taken never took place. As the war ended, bad news arrived, the certainty of the unthinkable horror: total annihilation.

An absence of several years and the absolute inability to communicate had produced a feeling of loss mixed with doubt. When the truth came up, after a long time, the memory, without a clear vision of the faces, without the voices, easily surrendered, mitigating the collective mourning. And for that reason, Mendel hadn't been able to cry. Then, ten years after the war, he was physically back, walking around the places where all had happened. He arrived at his street and found his house. He stopped. Recalling memories, he brought back all smiles, all caresses...

"Mendel, Mendel!," his grandmother calling. "Mendel, Mendel!," called Hanna, his *Yiddish mama*, serving the food and "demanding" him to eat. Then Mendel convulsively cried, an endless late cry, which overflew with each memory. Moishele touched his shoulder.

Suddenly, he calmed down. He placed the *tallit* his father gave him on his shoulders and prayed the *Kaddish* for all of them. It was October. It was *Rosh Hashanah*.[63] He gave a small *shofar*[64] to Moishele, who played it, as usual, marking the begin-

---

62 Nazi term, referring to their plan to annihilate the Jews.
63 Jewish New Year.
64 Jewish instrument most often made from a ram's horn, though it can also be made from the horn of a sheep or goat.

ning of a new year. In the *Rosh Hashanah* of 1942, 5716 on the Hebrew calendar, not a Jew from that place had his or her name written in the Book of Life.[65]

The sound of the *shofar* coming from the street caught the attention of a resident, who opened the windows. Surprised, a man about 60 years old started screaming, as if he had never seen anything like that:

"What is a Jew and a black boy doing in front of my house? And blowing this horn used in the synagogues? For sure, it's a joke!"

For over ten years, Ostrow had been *Judenfrei,*[66] as the Nazis used to say while telling their superiors that all Jews had been taken to concentration camps. The guy at the window asked the two strange figures to leave.

"Get out of here, you clowns! In Ostrow (don't you know?) the Jewish plague is over, we don't have Jews here anymore, not even fake ones like you, the Nazis had cleaned it all, I helped a little myself; no one lived to tell the tale, least of all at this house, I can assure you!"

"One lived, Wladislaw!" Mendel stated in Polish.

The little man shuddered. Widening his eyes, he stared for quite a long time at that man wearing a *kippah,* who said his name; and he felt dizzy when he recognized the person standing in front of his house, a Jew, a childhood friend. A woman came to "help" him; astonished, she quickly closed the window, but not before clearly listening to the voice outside, which was speaking on behalf of the ghosts who used to live there:

"Don't worry, I won't ask you to give my house back!"

Mendel walked away and started looking for the old Jewish cemetery. *I hope they have at least left the bones of our ancestors alone,* he thought. He entered the cemetery, but couldn't see any tombs; the tombstones have been removed and "recycled" for several uses. The place was now a soccer field. Young

---

65 Book containing the set of names of those who will remain alive for the year to come.
66 Nazi term, meaning "free of Jews."

Poles were running after a ball, even knowing that under that soil lay the remains of compatriots of different faith, who had escaped the Final Solution because they were "lucky" enough to be no longer alive when the SS arrived, Jews who didn't become smoke in the air in Treblinka.

He noticed that the Christian church didn't have a scratch, it was still intact on the top of the hill. But the synagogue of his *bar mitzvah*, with its yellow and blue stained glass windows, had become an unrecognizable wall, symbolically recalling the Wall in Jerusalem. In Ostrow, synagogues would never be destroyed again, simply because they didn't exist anymore, and none would ever be built again.

The human landscape at the once "Jewish Street" strongly contrasted to what it used to be: It now consisted of indifferent blond Poles, no longer of religious men with black, curly hair and their also black hats and overcoats — seen from the top, it looked like a runway of walking sunflowers.

Ah... the happy parades of the Hasidic orthodox, dancing and singing to the rhythm of the folk musicians called klezmer![67] Mendel couldn't think of Ostrow without "hearing" the bouncy sound of the clarinet.

The houses of the Jews had been robbed, not destroyed. Mendel pointed at each one of them, on the right and on the left, telling Moishele the names of the residents — none of them "was home":

"Yossef Aaronberg, his wife Esther and their kids Yaakov and Gimpel; Aaron Adler and his wife Malcha; Herschel Blumenshtok, his wife and their kids; Moshe Freedman, his wife Miriam and their kids Feytshe, Freida and Yaakov; Leybel Glatt, his wife Ruth and their son Chaim; Yaakov Fogel, his wife Dvora and their kids, Hinde, Toby, Pessel, Shmuel, David and Yosef; Eliezer Glazman, his wife Sheyndel Yechit and their kids Aaron, Bella, Reyzel and Tami; Blyme Dikerman and his brothers Leybel and Itzchak; the family Freyberg; Yaakov Feld-

---

67 A traditionally itinerant Jewish folk musician of Eastern Europe performing in a small band.

man, his wife and their kids; Pinchas Erman, his wife Dvora and their kids; Aaron Katz and his wife Rivka; Eliezer Mayer, his wife Etta-Hanna and their kids Miriam, Shlomo, Sima, Bluma and Mina; Mordechai Weiss, his wife Perele and their kids Malcha-Rachel and Zalman-Hirash; Moshe Weintraub and his wife Sheva; Pinchas Weinberg, his wife Chana and their daughter Alta; Reuben Weissberg, his wife Tzipora and their kids Yente, Leah, Feyge and Tsirel..."

He stopped in front of a house. Moishele noticed some pain on his face, but didn't ask anything. Mendel remained in heavy silence; he didn't talk about it, or rather, didn't talk about whom was related to that place. It was the house of Rebecca, his ex-fiancée, who inexplicably killed herself with poison, at a calm time, before the German invasion. The reason was never known, maybe a mental illness not known at the time. She had an unsettled behavior, sometimes happy, sometimes introverted.

Ironically, his fiancée's suicide was one the factors which had contributed to save his life. Mendel had left Ostrow and emigrated to Brazil to run away from that bitter memory, and that way he had escaped going to Treblinka. Also concerning Rebecca, there was nothing left, not even her *matzeiva*,[68] which had been stolen by marble looters, birds of prey who hooked their claws in the remains left by the swastika.

Mendel experienced another great commotion while he was passing by a shed. He saw, inside the place, an enormous quantity of old sewing machines, packed one on the top of another, with a sign saying "saved from fire," and being sold for peanuts. Mendel didn't have any doubt where they had come from. In Ostrow, being a tailor was very common among the Jews, who also worked for the rich Poles, tailoring their daily garments and party outfits, a "clientele" who, later, would refuse to give any kind of help and mocked at their pain; many of them even cooperated with the executioners. *What about the*

---

68 Hebrew word for "tombstone."

shoemakers? Where did hundreds of hammers go? Maybe, to a German weapon factory.

Mendel couldn't resist. He walked around that "concentration camp" of inanimate things, which, one day, had depended on the lives of its users to be "alive" as well. He moved slowly, as if walking through a cemetery. Each piece was a memorial. *How many unfinished orders would have been abruptly interrupted?* He used to know all the tailors in town. The sound of sewing machines was a symphony in Ostrow during the day and parts of dawn, including at his house, where his grandfather also lived.

Suddenly, something impressively improbable happened. Mendel saw what could have been his grandfather sewing machine, due to two worn letters in the name: the first S and the last R. He wasn't sure, but he decided to open the first drawer anyway. It was empty. Then, the second. Couldn't find anything. But when he opened the third drawer, he almost had a heart attack: He found the picture of a boy wearing short pants — it was him, in the picture his grandfather kept there to take a look and soften tiredness; according to the season, the two would play together, sledding or playing ball.

Meanwhile, the guard was looking at him without understanding why someone would be interested in such old, rusty stuff; he was following the movements of that unusual "client," trying to imagine where he had come from... He hasn't seen a man wearing a *kippah* for a long time, since the last ones on the train platform.

Mendel, without hesitating, put the picture in his pocket. It belonged to him.

The images of the workers, both men and women, carpenters carrying doors and windows on their shoulders, girls humming, sitting in front of a counter while bundling brooms, the noisy small traders... Everything he had learned would change the history of his life. Until this return, he barely knew that his family had been executed. But now he had learned how, it had been possible to reconstitute, step-by-step, the itinerary of the annihilation: The formation of the ghetto, the hunger, diseases such as starvation and typhus, the railroad transport to "work camps"… until the final goal, the execution.

For how long would this new memory allow him to live as he had been living up to that moment? Before, he had organically resisted the absence of the missing, but the apocalyptic echo remained, not so much before his eyes and ears, but in his heart and soul. He "saw," "heard" and, above all, "felt."

For a moment, he thought about going to Treblinka, the Nazi concentration camp the population of his city was sent to, but he really didn't want to turn this into a real memory. It was time to go, to leave Ostrow again, as he had done thirty years before.

He didn't buy any souvenirs, not even a postcard. He didn't want to take anything palpable from that place. At the same station, he would take the train to Warsaw. From there, by airplane, he would go to Rome, and, finally, return to Brazil.

Still on the train, awaiting the departure, something else happened. Sitting by the window, Moishele told Mendel that, on the platform, at a short distance, a man wearing a *kippah* was staring at them.

"A man wearing a *kippah*? Where?" the anxious and incredulous Mendel asked. Obviously, he wasn't a resident of the city.

"There!" Moishele pointed.

"Where, where?"

Moishele kept pointing in the same direction, but Mendel couldn't see anyone.

"Is he still there?" Mendel insisted.

"Yes!"

The platform was empty, but Mendel knew Moishele was not the type of boy who would joke about such things.

"How does he look like?"

"Tall, skin, a bit bald…"

"Is he wearing glasses?"

"Yes."

"How are his glasses?"

"A clear lens and another dark, covering his left eye. He probably doesn't have this eye."

Mendel was quiet for a while, lowered his head and quietly prayed. Then, he said:

"It's my father!"

The train whistles went off and they started to move.

7. THE *DYBBUK*

Since he came back from his trip, Mendel was an unhealthy man. He had Ostrow in his spirit; he couldn't distinguish if he was at home or had left his home in Poland. He didn't witness part of the Holocaust who annihilated his city, relatives and friends, but, shortly ago, he had been there. Due to fate's mistake, he was physically intact, saved by the impact of his fiancée suicide and by the lack of hope to stay in the boundaries of the Jewish zone, facts that motivated him to emigrate. He philosophized: *So, that's how life goes... it is a roulette: Rebecca's sacrifice helped me slip away from the Nazis...*

The second memory he had brought with him had become a living and lasting nightmare. The Jews who emigrated hadn't returned to their places of origin neither suffered the shock of an imaginary reunion with so many dead people; they had been carrying a ten-year mourning — as they heard about the Holocaust in 1945, when the war was over —, living with a possible serenity that only time can bring. But Mendel's mourning had, somehow, painfully restarted.

He has changed a lot. He was another person, unrecognizable, revolted, getting angry over nothing. Frequently asked, he wasn't motivated to talk about the usual wonders of the trip, nothing about Paris, nothing about the Eiffel Tower, nothing about the Arch of Triumph, nothing about the changing of the guard in London. Concerning Faiga, he simply gave her the camera and asked her to develop the pictures. In Ostrow, he hadn't taken any pictures. Moishele was the one with the task of describing the touristic points, the city details, what they had seen and eaten in each place.

What could have been the reason for such visible transformation? Moishele was well aware, and even knew the name of that "metamorphosis": Ostrow!

Mendel kept getting worse. His usual sweetness concerning simple things had given way to a hostile and aggressive personality. He refused to eat, broke plates and didn't want to see anyone. He ended up locking himself in the bedroom, barely opening the door to get some food, up to the point that, very weak, he could no longer get up.

Frightened, Faiga called a doctor who used to attend at a two-story house next to the drugstore. With a spare key, she opened the bedroom's door, but Mendel didn't allow the doctor to examine him, he cursed and tried to scratch him. He would answer to any question in a furious way, speaking a strange language. The doctor was sure it was a psychiatric problem and recommended a specialist. The diagnosis didn't take long: Mendel was losing his "mental faculties."

"It is necessary to hospitalize him," the doctor stated.

Faiga came closer to his bed and the doctor asked her to ask him his name. Mendel answered in Yiddish, but not with his normal voice. With a guttural, unrecognizable, threatening voice, and sounding like a woman, he said:

"I'm Rebecca, Mendel's fiancée!"

Faiga stepped back. She was aware of Mendel's history; on the ship, he had told her the whole story about the suicide. When she tried to come closer, she was pushed away, called a whore and a bitch. "It isn't him in that bed," she said. What or whoever it was, the voice was repeating that it was his fiancée, and that she had returned to take him.

Realizing that Mendel was noticeably languishing and

spent days without any improvement, Faiga, frightened by the condition of her husband, who was transformed into a kind of monster, besides considering the doctors' inability to do something and without knowing what else to do, decided to talk to Rabbi Meyer. After listening to the story about Mendel's fiancée, the religious man promptly suspected it could be a *dybbuk*, a bad spirit.

He had heard about a similar case in Lithuania: On her wedding day, a young woman had her body taken by the spirit of her ex-fiancé; they weren't able to "free" her and she ended up dead. Concerning Mendel, it was the contrary: The spirit of an ex-fiancée was trying to take her ex-fiancé's soul. He consulted the chapters of the *Talmud* related to this topic and separated suitable prayers; in the following day, he went to Mendel's house to try to help him.

He was quickly taken to the possessed's room, where he bent down and asked in Yiddish:

"Who are you?"

The answer, in the same language, only included offenses. Rabbi Meyer insisted.

"Who are you?"

"I'm Rebecca, Mendel's fiancée!" the creature answered, mocking the religious man.

Shaking, the Rabbi called Faiga:

"It's a *dybbuk*, I have no doubts."

Faiga cried; she was desperate. She knew it was a *dybbuk*, an evil tormented spirit, who "gets into" the body of a person, and does whatever it takes to bring the person with him.

The Rabbi decided to get some reinforcement and went to the synagogue, where a group of religious men was constantly praying. Breathless, he had barely stepped on the sidewalk when he bumped into the Spanish Priest of the local parish, who was walking by. With the impact, both almost fell to the ground. Such improbable meeting enabled a not less improbable dialog between the two theological "opponents":

"What's the rush? Where's the fire?" the Priest asked.

"It was God who sent you!" the Rabbi answered, surprising the Priest.

"Have you lost your mind? Can't you see I have a cassock on? And you with this black overcoat, hat, long beard... you must be a Rabbi, right?"

"It's true. I'm a Rabbi."

The Priest was ironic:

"So, if you don't mind my asking, why God would send a Priest to talk to a Rabbi?"

"You're right, but we know God writes straight with crooked lines!" the Jew argued.

"Assuming you're right, what has God written with crooked lines this time?" the Priest continued.

"It's a matter of life and death!" the Rabbi shouted.

"But Christ was crucified over two thousand years ago, you know that better than me," the Priest provoked.

"I'm not joking. It's about a case of exorcism!" the Rabbi added.

"Well, if it's against the devil, we can talk," the Priest gave in, agreeing to a deal against the common enemy.

Prepared as if they were going to a war, the Priest was informed that the case involved a *dybbuk*, who is not a fallen angel, but produces similar effects on the incorporated.

Priest Alonso — that was the name of the Christian Iberian clerical — ran to the sacristy and quickly returned, "armed" with a powerful arsenal: thuribles, sprinkler and Holy water, and an "Exorcism Manual" as well. The Rabbi had only the small and tuned ram horn, the *shofar*.

Together, they went up the stairs and entered the house, conducted by the astonished Faiga, who could barely believe what she was seeing: A Rabbi and a Priest in concert with each other to face a *dybbuk*. In Poland, such scene would be inconceivable.

They were standing, one on each side of the bed. The Rabbi, authoritarian, was uttering watchwords taken from the *Talmud*, ordering the invader to immediately leave the body of that pure man, sometimes in Yiddish, sometimes in Hebrew. On the left side of the bed, Priest Alonso sprinkled Holy Water and impregnated the place with incense. And, of course, also ordered the evil intruder to leave, according to the instructions of his religion, very similar, in this case, to the Jewish methodology.

"Begone, Satan!" the Priest repeated, relentlessly.

But even with all the attention and distance, they couldn't escape the agility of the *dybbuk*, who, indifferent to the watchwords, slapped both, on the right and on the left, and told them to go to the depths in Yiddish and Spanish, respectively.

Repeated and useless attempts took the ecumenical partnership to exhaustion. The *dybbuk* was getting stronger, and Mendel weaker. Faiga's care and effort to put some food down Mendel's throat were also unsuccessful. It was all given back over her white dress, mixed to a greenish liquid that looked like pea soup. *For how long would her poor husband resist the "indissoluble presence" of the ex-fiancée, who, screaming and frightening everybody, didn't yield an inch concerning her evil goal of getting her fiancé back, taking him out of this world?*

At this time, heartbroken, Faiga agreed to tie her unfortunate husband with powerful ties on his hands and feet. Called to the endeavor, two very strong "specialists" of a sanatorium were not enough. They asked, then, the help of two more friends, and, two hours later, the service was concluded.

But the immobilization of the possessed didn't solve the problem. Mendel was considered already lost, ready to succumb; no medicine or rabbinic-clerical battle could free him from the claws of the evil spirit. They still counted on the fragile prayers of their friends, the regulars at the synagogue, who, being sure Mendel was strongly tied, would regularly stop by.

Time was running. Wrapped in hopelessness, Faiga already showed signs of acceptance, the kind of acceptance in which you believe what would be "the best" for the beloved person, even if this "best" is not accepted by common sense. She had tried everything, including reputable doctors, specialists, an exorcist Rabbi and an exorcist Priest. She had used up all sources, physical and metaphysical. She was ready to be alone in this world, and the only thing that kept her from being desperate was Moishele's support.

Vicentina had traveled to Bahia[69] to celebrate the 2nd of February, Iemanjá's Day. On her return, she found that grotesque scene: Her boss tied to a bed, being reluctant and angrily swearing at anyone who would come closer. She quickly realized that Mendel wouldn't resist for too long.

"It's an *encosto*,"[70] she stated.

Faiga couldn't understand, and Moishele explained to her the common points between a *dybbuk* and an *encosto*. Vicentina decided to act fast. She ran to her room and came back wearing white clothes, as an yialorisha.[71] She asked Faiga to leave the room and signalized Moishele to take her outside. He quickly understood what his mother was about to do.

Vicentina faced the fury of the *dybbuk*. In trance, her voice changed, it was masculine and strong; she faced and answered back all the curses, and covered "Rebecca" in cigar smoke. Outside the room, it was possible to hear the noisy confrontation, it sounded like a desperate battle between a beast and its relentless hunter. But, little by little, the intensity of the battle was allaying. It was necessary to put the ear against the door to hear something.

The *dybbuk* was agonizing. The toes of the imprisoned were shaking. It was a Kabbalistic sign of retreat. The battle was over, and Mendel fell into a deep sleep. His face looked finally relieved.

He woke up in the next morning. He was free. How could they explain to him a long and unnoticed gap in the calendar, a time which his mind and body weren't aware of? They agreed to tell him he had had very high fever, caused by a virus.

"I got this virus during the trip," Mendel said, without

---

69 State located in the Eastern region of Brazil.
70 Spirit of a dead person in *Umbanda*.
71 The highest female authority in a *terreiro*.

knowing he was right about the geographical origin, but not about the responsible agent.

For a while, the drama was kept as a secret. Nobody told him he was taken by a *dybbuk*, according to Faiga, or by an *encosto*, according to Vicentina. And he kept not knowing what had happened to him until he ran into Priest Alonso, one of the exorcists who tried to help him, without success.

Mendel was physically recovered and looking good. The Priest discreetly came towards him.

"Sorry for asking, but weren't you sick? Didn't you have problems… psychological problems?" he was running around the bush.

Mendel naturally answered:

"It's true, I was very sick, an infection that attacked my head. I spent many days asleep until the fever diminished."

"And can't you remember anything? The people around, the doctors who examined you?"

"I know there had been many doctors, but I can't remember any of them."

Moved by an irresistible curiosity, the Priest was about to reveal the secret agreed upon at Mendel's house; nobody could possibly imagine that the unaware Priest would run into the "newly-exorcized."

"Mister Mendel, I really must ask you a question about your illness."

Mendel felt as he didn't have anything to hide.

"Of course! Be my guest, I'm grateful for your interest!" Mendel said, and joked:

"You… all this interest about my health… you're not trying to turn me into a new-Christian, are you?"

The priest laughed, and also joked:

"During the Inquisition your 'disease' would have taken you to the bonfire."

Mendel was still at ease:

"Poor me, what have I done?"

"You haven't done anything. I'm talking about the *dyb-buk*. What happened to it?"

"*Dybbuk*?"

Mendel frowned. A Priest talking about a *dybbuk*... That was way too weird!

The Priest explained:

"One day, in front of your home, I ran into the Rabbi, who asked for my help. Of course, I couldn't understand the kind of help a Rabbi would want from a Priest. He told me, then, that it was a case of exorcism, that he couldn't remove the *dybbuk*, an evil spirit, from the body of a Jew who lived in that house. Of course, I couldn't have said no. I went to your room and saw something horrible, something I'd never seen before: You were screaming in a different voice, I had no idea what that voice was, man or woman, swearing at everybody, you desperately tried to leave the bed and were throwing up a greenish liquid. I had no doubts, you were possessed by the devil. I ran to my church and came back with a thurible, a sprinkler and my exorcism book. Then, the Rabbi and I, each with his own liturgy, started trying to free you from the *dybbuk*, that I'm used to call a different name. But the name doesn't matter. What I can tell you is that the more we struggled, the more aggressive you, I mean, the *dybbuk,* was, up to the point of punching me and the Rabbi on the face."

Mendel couldn't believe the Priest. He thought it was a bad joke, until he heard him saying:

"The bad spirit even had a human name! It's one of the devil's tricks, assuming the identity he pleases. This one had a woman's name, it said it was Rebecca, your ex-fiancée, and that she had come to take you."

At this moment, a simple and nice reunion between neighbors started making Mendel nervous. His mention of that name meant something was being hidden, there was something he didn't know. It couldn't have been only a coincidence. He had to find out what really happened during the period he was "unconscious."

The dybbuk, Priest Alonso, Rebecca, the Rabbi Meyer... All these had created an aura of uncertainty: *So, was it really a fever? Or a more violent kind of virus?* At the same time, associating the facts, he remembered standing in front of Rebecca's house for quite a while in Ostrow... It was impossible, *dybbuks* don't exist, they were sort of a Jewish folklore. *So that was the reason my family kept me unaware of all the facts*, he concluded.

He tried to think of a subtle way of finding the truth without showing he was already aware of it. The next day, he invited Moishele to have some ice cream at the neighborhood square. They seated on one of those pleasant benches, under a big, tall tree. While having ice cream, pretending to be at ease, Mendel brought up the subject and threw the bait:

"Did you know, Moishele, that I was possessed by a *dybbuk*?"

Moishele was paralyzed. What should he say? Mendel was asking as if he was already aware of everything. But how? They had agreed to keep secret all the facts about his "illness." He pretended he didn't understand the question.

Mendel, looking at his ice cream, continued:

"*Dybbuk*... A spirit that gets into our body and doesn't want to leave. It makes us sick, violent and gradually weaker."

Moishele gave in:

"Who told you that, Mendel? My mother and Mrs. Faiga agreed, for your own good, not to mention such horrible thing..."

"How horrible?"

Moishele hesitated. He didn't want to shock Mendel by describing what he had seen. But Mendel insisted; he said he was fine, but he really needed to know what had happened while he was unconscious. And he added that all this story about a *dybbuk* was pure folklore, from centuries ago, nobody would take it seriously anymore.

Moishele, then, described his pathological condition from the very beginning: Deeply depressed, evolving to an uncontrolled agressiveness, a croaky voice, which sounded like a man or a woman, who said it was Rebecca and had come to take her fiancé; and the endless visits of many frightened doctors, who couldn't do anything, the attempt of the Rabbi and the Priest, after agreeing it was an exorcism case. Not even the *shofar* worked.

Mendel listened to everything in silence. He didn't mind getting more information. He thought about Faiga. *How could she handle these horror days? Doctors, nurses from a sanatorium, an unusual partnership between a Priest and a Rabbi... The husband turning in bed as a beast tied to the bed. Yes, Sir, what a great show!* And the worst, the lack of an accurate medical diagnosis. Someone had even suggested a name for all that: hysteria.

Definitely, it was better to pretend nothing had happened. The problem was the mouthy Priest. *If people from the neighborhood start giving me a funny look, I'll know the news is around: the Jew had the devil in him!* He would have to move to a different neighborhood. And if the Rabbi broke the secret? He would be mocked at Praça Onze: "Mendel, how is your *dybbuk* fiancée?"

He couldn't believe it; how could he believe it in the 20th century?

Without apparent reason, Mendel had taken off one of his shoes and sock, and was staring at the tip of his toes. He couldn't believe what he was doing: According to an old Jewish belief, the *dybbuk* leaves the person's body through the feet, leaving tiny blood spots on the tip of the toes. *Medieval ignorance, of course!* He put the shoe back and felt like a fool. There was nothing to check.

"Why did you do that?" Moishele asked.

"What?"

"You took your shoe and sock off and were examining your toes."

There was not a chance Mendel would answer that question. He would feel too ridiculous, so he made up a reason:

"A sort of allergy, it was bothering me."

"On the tip of your toes?"

"Yes. But it's gone now."

"Curious..."

"Why?"

Moishele told him everything that had happened, including Vicentina's arrival, the way she was dressed, all in white, the locked door. Then, the scaring noise coming from inside and, suddenly, the silence. It was over. She opened the door and Mendel was calmly sleeping, free from the ties.

"But what have all these to do with me taking off my shoe and looking at my feet?" Mendel wanted to know, feeling a bit nervous.

Moishele explained:

"As soon as we entered the room, Mrs. Faiga ran to check your toes."

Now, more than nervous, Mendel was truly anxious.

"Why has she done that?"

"She said the evil spirit was gone, because there were some little spots of blood on your toes. 'That's from where the *dybbuk* had left,' she said."

Mendel was quiet, because he had heard many times, in Ostrow, "that's how the *dybbuk* leaves." And no one ever talked about *dybbuks* again. It didn't take Mendel long to forget all he was told. He, himself, couldn't remember anything, as he was anesthetized all the time. But he kept thinking: *A Rabbi and a Priest together to exorcise me... That's absurd! No one had ever heard of such thing; and all to no avail, they were even beaten by the dybbuk!*

Not having a logical explanation made him uncomfortable, and he was searching for a suitable answer related to the current century. He tried talking to one of the doctors who had examined him, also a Jew, Dr. Bernard Garbasky:

"Doctor, please, tell me what happened to me. Did I have a madness attack? I get worried only thinking about it."

"As soon as I saw you, I thought about a violent hysterical attack, or even schizophrenia. The first thing I tried was to make you sleep, you were extremely violent, I had never seen a patient with such ferocity, you wanted to beat everyone; inexplicably, you said you were your ex-fiancée Rebecca who had come to take her fiancé... It was not a normal voice."

Mendel was straight to the point:

"Yes, doctor, but what was your diagnosis?"

"To be honest, whatever you had doesn't fit any diagnosis, it's close to hysteria, but not at this degree. I also talked to other doctors who examined you."

"And what have they said?"

"They agreed with me. No one could come to a conclusion, except..."

"Except?"

"Never mind. It was not a doctor, don't take it too seriously."

"Yes... but who are you talking about?"

"My mother, a Polish Jew, an immigrant like you; without mentioning names, I told her about your case."

Staring at the doctor, Mendel was, actually, more anxious about the mother's opinion than about the doctor's prognosis.

"And what has she said?"

Joking and laughing, the doctor made a funny horror face, and said:

"She said it was a *DYBBUK!*"

Mendel pretended he was also laughing, and quickly left the doctor's office.

The next day, he looked for the Rabbi and asked for a prayer for his ex-fiancée, Rebecca.

8. Moishele's High School

Moishele had finished middle school and was about to start high school; after that, he intended to go to college. He attended the Graduation Mass and didn't feel as a fish out of water in the Christian church, although he didn't feel as comfortable as he used to feel in the *terreiro* and in the synagogue. His faith wasn't clannish, he was able to find answers and support in the three religions. He didn't even think about adopting one, or being adopted by any of them. Mendel, who didn't appreciate any exaggeration nearing fanaticism and thought the proselytism of faith was embarrassing, had been raising him that way. Once, Moishele "illegally" got into a confessional and enjoyed the novelty, but he omitted the fact that he wasn't baptized. He ended up confessing those things all teenagers are motivated to confess, emphasizing sexual topics — "reading" erotic magazines, masturbation and so on. Without understanding the reason for such strange interrogation, Moishele, without prior notification, abandoned the small place and his confessor. Due to shyness, he hadn't talked to anyone about his experience.

He had also learned with Mendel that God, even using different names, is only one. Concerning the *Umbanda*, there was no conflict, as the syncretism cleverly smoothed the rough edges of faith and devotion. In addition, the history of creation in the *Torah,* the Old Testament, was common ground for several religions. But as his social life started, Moishele found it necessary to give an answer to the question which, in those years, was frequently asked: "What's your religion?"

He couldn't say Jew, Christian or *Umbandista* without lying. Least of all, say he practiced three religions, or none. For that reason, he was practical. He said he was Christian just to avoid strangeness, paying lip service, because people normally asked that without really caring, as you ask about one's favorite soccer team or food.

Concerning his girlfriends, for external effect, he was a Christian on a daily basis. If some of them asked him to attend the Sunday Mass, he could do it naturally. In the beginning, he copied the movements and repeated what he listened, including the entry at the Holy Water sink and the last song of praise. He ended up learning the order of the liturgy, and was keen on contributing to the Money Basket. He wasn't moved by the informality of the Mass, but, eventually, enjoyed the sermons preached by an old Priest, who always provoked those who "hoard treasures upon Earth." He decided to ask Mendel if it was about the money kept in the safety box or at the bank.

At his new school, during the first class, he was truly impressed by the personality of his Physics teacher, a young man who was also black and spoke with undoubted confidence; you couldn't possibly sleep during his classes. After explaining the program, he informed the theme of the following class, in fact, the first one: The Origin of the Universe.

Very excited about the new subject, Moishele told Mendel he had a black teacher, and that he had really enjoyed his class. Before, he considered this subject to be the "bogeyman," according to his colleagues. But Mr. Amauri made him feel calm, and anxious for the next classes as well.

"What will it be about?" Mendel asked.

"Mr. Amauri will explain the origin of the Universe."

"It's not that hard! You can find it in the *Torah!*" Mendel added.

"But it's not a religion class, it's Physics."

"It doesn't matter. Everyone knows, even the Christians, that God made the world in six days and rested on the seventh day. That's why we have the Sabbath, the day of rest," Mendel concluded, incisively.

"I didn't quite understand, but he mentioned a great explosion at the beginning of everything," Moishele remarked.

Mendel, curious, was thinking about this so-called explosion. *What explosion would it be? I think Moishele misunderstood it; the teacher, for sure, will talk about the atomic bomb, created by Einstein, who was a Jew as well.*

Just in case, Mendel reread the Genesis, but couldn't find anything about such novelty.

The following class, when Mr. Amauri said the Universe was a result of the Big Bang, the explosion of a small ball full of energy, which spread throughout space creating the planets and the stars, Moishele smiled, as he thought he was joking. When he finally got convinced it was a scientific theory, he didn't express his disbelief right away. He felt like running home and telling Mendel: "An explosion! Totally nonsense!"

The teacher also added that the Universe was ready in three seconds, with all stars and galaxies. *So, there was nothing about six days of divine work, nothing about resting on Saturday, nor on Sunday...* And, to increase his disappointment, he looked around and noticed the other students were spellbound by the news. *How could the explosion of a small ball be so big?* Moishele copied the formula the teacher wrote on the blackboard:

$E = mc^2$.

When he told Mendel what he had learned, Moishele expected him to be indignant. However, the moment he heard that the theory of an explosion creating the Universe was based on a formula developed by Einstein, a Jew, Mendel was silent. He thought, *if Einstein said it, it surely had gravitas.* In any case, he wasn't worried. Einstein had never said anything against the Sabbath.

Moishele was puzzled. There was Mendel, in front of

him, accepting the world could be the result of the explosion of a small ball. Refusing to accept it, and more than that, disoriented, he talked to Vicentina, and asked her to intervene in the matter, asking the orishas to "put some light" in the teacher's head — even being black, with roots in Africa, Mr. Amauri was defending a new and absurd theory related to the creation of the Earth.

He didn't find any support. Vicentina chose not to get involved in such subject; she only said it was a "white people thing" and that the teacher, being black, shouldn't interfere with it.

"The orishas created and rule the world."

Entangled in the sacred principles of the multiple religious faith he built himself, using Jewish, *Umbandista* and Christian "cement," after that class about the *Big Bang* Moishele was changing little by little. He started thinking, questioning and doubting...

"Mendel," he insisted, "Do you really think it happened that way? That an explosion had originated the Universe?"

"Moishele, are you still thinking about it? The scientists can say whatever crosses their minds, and, then, they call it a 'theory'; after all, they get paid for that. How God created the world will always remain a mystery, there are so many significant things that remain a mystery." And he continued, speaking as a teacher: "Nobody knows the Coca-Cola formula, for example, it's a secret the manufacturers keep under lock and key."

"And what has Coca-Cola to do with the creation of the world?"

"Well, Moishele, if not even the owners of Coca-Cola reveal how it's made, do you think God will be around telling how he made the Universe?"

For some time, Moishele's young brain balanced the ancient Jewish wisdom, adapted by Mendel to Coca-Cola, with the modern scientific wisdom brought to the classroom. It was 1952. The Big Bang theory was only two years old.

Mendel and Moishele loved each other as father and son,

and Mendel enjoyed all the scientific novelties Moishele brought home from school. In Poland, he had mainly studied in non-official schools, home schools in which the *melamed*, the teacher, only taught topics related to religion. Later, he had studied secular subjects in a public school implemented by the government in his town, but only for two years. Now, accompanying the student Moishele, he felt as a student himself, and his curiosity was insatiable; he kept asking for explanations about the Big Bang. At a particular time, the scientific revelation started to be confronted with what he had studied at the Reb Avrum's *cheder*,[72] where he learned to pray and memorize parts of the *Torah*. The paradox science versus religion was slowly getting into his mind. Even his wife noticed he had been distracted: Before going to bed, sometimes, he forgot the usual prayer or to wear his *kippah*.

"What's happening, Mendel? Are you worried about anything?" Faiga wanted to know.

"It's something they taught at Moishele's school."

"Anything against the Jews?"

"No... Something to do with Einstein," Mendel started explaining what he "knew."

"Einstein? Einstein, who?"

"Come on, Faiga, don't you know who Albert Einstein is?"

"That Yid related to the atomic bomb?"

"*Yo, yo...*[73] the Yid of the atomic bomb," Mendel agreed, using Ashkenazi slang.

"And what has he done this time? An even more powerful bomb?"

"I heard he has been teaching that there was a great explosion, called the Big Bang, which created the whole world."

"The whole world?"

"Yes... All the stars, all the planets, the Earth, the moon, the sun..."

---

72 Home religious school in the *shtetl*, Jewish settlement in Eastern Europe.
73 "Yes, yes" in Yiddish.

"Don't be a fool! How can you believe such thing? Only because he's a Yid do you have to believe all he says? For me, he's *meshugge*, with that tongue sticking out."

"I need to talk to the Rabbi. If what Moishele's teacher said is true, if God created the world in a short minute, so He didn't need to rest."

"So?"

"If He didn't rest, so the Sabbath, which is our day of rest, also doesn't exist, although Einstein hasn't mentioned anything about it."

"Yankel will love hearing about it, he's always complaining about missing the Saturday fair," Faiga concluded.

Since he heard about the Big Bang, guided by Moishele, Mendel was paying closer attention to the sky. He contemplated the stars and digressed into the concept of the beginning of everything, trying to find a link between the Genesis and Mr. Amauri's class. One thing led to another, and he ended up buying the telescope Moishele wanted. He was amazed when he "found" the rings of Saturn, and the Milky Way made him speechless. Without realizing, he was becoming an empirical "man of science."

Moishele, carrying an Astronomy map, turned him into his witness during their cosmic incursions. However, when Mendel heard that the dust in the Milky Way, dotted with "diamonds," was nothing more than a swarm of billions of stars, he had a relapse: *My apologies to Einstein, but that can't be the result of an explosion, or whatever it is.* And that night, tranquilizing Faiga, he became the "old" Mendel again. He prayed with a great feeling of regret, asking for forgiveness for doubting the Sabbath.

Moishele was walking the other way. His multiple spiritual references had acquired faded colors. He studied Galileo, who wasn't crucified, but was actually demanded by the church to disown his revolutionary discovery, according to which the Earth was not the center of the Universe, and rotated around the sun. Copernicus, Giordano Bruno and Newton were his new prophets, his new saints, his new orishas. He memorized and knew "a bit" about all the planets, according to their distance from the sun: Mercury, Venus, Earth, Mars, Jupiter, Saturn, Uranus, Neptune and Pluto.

Other subjects in the program also led him to the opposite side of the immaterial caress of religions, as the strong wind moves the navigator away from his safe haven. An eccentric "Moral and Civic" teacher instilled some socialist ideas in their minds, "religion is the opium of the people." He explained this "opium effect": It promised happiness in a different world; it didn't matter being poor here on Earth, the person's mission must be the guarantee of eternal happiness, but only in heaven. As the catechists, he insisted on the saying: "Property is theft." Later this teacher was fired from the old Ateneu Barbosa de Oliveira, Moishele's school, but he had already done some damage to Moishele's head. The young man started to address religion in a totally different way, not a nice one; and, by himself, related the knowledge acquired during those classes to the slaves' condition, including his grandparents and all the captives owned by someone: "If all property is theft, every slave master is a thief." He was congratulated for such brilliant and logical conclusion, and enjoyed the level of intimacy demonstrated by the teacher, who hugged him and called him "buddy."

Moishele was sad to hear the teacher was fired. Some parents complained, saying he was a communist, and, to avoid risks, the director of the school hired a retired military officer to take his place. Twenty years later, Moishele saw the teacher in a picture, among "subversive" people who had been exchanged for a kidnapped ambassador.

The faculty was divided concerning the dismissal of the teacher, and would, once again, be on opposite sides in a tense episode, which was triggered by a confrontation between Mr. Alencar and his black student.

9. The Confrontation

At school, Moishele, for the first time, had contact with an authentic and explicit manifestation of anti-Semite racism. Alencar, the History teacher, used to be a member of the Brazilian Integralism Movement, which expressed itself in the 1930's and 40's, with strong infiltration in the military and among renowned intellectuals, mirroring the fascist ideal.

During a class about World War II — there was no reference to the fact in the History book used in school —, Alencar sadistically talked about the concentration camps to which the Jews were taken and executed in gas chambers: "Millions of Jews were executed all over Europe!" And asked the class, using a cruel and degrading joke: "Do you know how the Jews left the concentration camps?" And he answered himself, laughing: "Through the chimney! All Jacobs, Isaacs and Saras were put into incinerators and became smoke!"

Until that day, Moishele had never been discriminated for being black; but he was deeply hurt by that "lesson" about the Jews. Absurdly, Mr. Alencar didn't consider the slaughtering of the Jews a tragedy, and he made his opinion clear. As he transformed that in a joke, Moishele could realize the Nazis' ideology had left its seeds, even there, in that school, in that classroom, less than a decade after the Holocaust.

What happened after that was something absolutely unpredictable. Two Jew students in the classroom lowered their heads. Hurt and powerless, they didn't react, they were quiet and even embarrassed about the looks and mocking laughs of some colleagues. Moishele, however, couldn't stand it, and reacted explosively. He felt the humiliation, not only due to his sympathy for the executed, but for himself. His "Jewish blood" boiled.

He stood up, revolted, and didn't mince the words. He screamed very loud at Alencar:

"If it were your mother leaving through the chimney, would you be joking about it?"

There was a commotion in the classroom; then, all the voices fell silent. An instant hatred made the teacher blush, and all the wide opened eyes of the students stared at him. The violent reaction of a black boy defending the Jews, the way Moishele did, bewildered Alencar. He couldn't understand the reason, neither find any logic concerning that attitude — a black boy taking up the cudgels for the Jews was something new for him, he had never seen anything like that before.

The environment, filled with anger, indicated confusion. There was a challenge in the air. Alencar realized he had crossed the line, made a serious gaffe through an unnecessary outburst, which showed his controversial ideological tendency. Moishele's reaction had put him on the spot, on the verge of demoralization.

He had to be drastic. And he was. He asked Moishele to leave the classroom and talk to the principal.

Moishele got a two-day suspension. He had never been discriminated for the color of his skin, and, then, ironically, he had been punished for expressing repugnance concerning the mockery about an assimilated feeling. During these two days, he had strange nightmares; he dreamed he was a slave on the quarterdeck of a slave ship, being whipped by the Nazis from the SS.

When he told Mendel what had happened, that he had

been suspended for reacting against Alencar's mockery, he expected him to be shocked and react, as he was directly connected to the offense. *Mendel wouldn't remain passive*, he thought, *they would go together to the principal's office and denounce the prejudice* — ironically, prejudice coming from a History teacher, who had been aware of the recent executions in the concentration camps in Eastern Europe.

Mendel, however, didn't show he was disgusted. On the contrary, he remained quiet; he was aware of the principal's injustice, but wasn't willing to protest; he didn't show his wrath because the situation didn't surprise him. For centuries, sometimes motivated by religion, sometimes by racial issues, the sons of the *Torah* have never lived in peace. The teacher's "comment" in the classroom was like a lost spike, the kind that frequently escapes from great fires. He couldn't count how many times, even in public places, he had heard loose sentences such as "Hitler should have exterminated all of them!"

Moishele, on the other hand, didn't carry such atavistic and conformist heritage in his soul. He had the spirit of a warrior, and couldn't understand such conformism. After all, short time ago, in Poland, they had seen the remaining signs of the savagery; they had been there, stepped on the soil where it all had happened. He thought about "fighting," but without Mendel, that would be impossible. He had to patiently wait for the end of his suspension.

He was able to catch up with the classes he missed, as his colleagues helped him. But what really hurt was the pain of injustice, and he talked to his mother about it. Vicentina listened quietly, and didn't say anything. She didn't have to. Moishele knew her well, her eyes were saying everything... At the right time, his orisha would light the way he should follow.

As the suspension was over, Moishele ran back to school, anxious to return to his classes; he would attend the History class as nothing had happened, and was hoping the teacher would do the same. But he was stopped at the gate by the inspector, who took him to the principal's office. Then, he heard he hadn't been only suspended. Under pressure from Alencar, who was strongly supported in the political spheres due to his past involvement in the Integralism Movement, the principal, who also took part — with less influence — in the fascist movement, told Moishele he had been expelled from school.

Moishele held back his tears until he got home. Mendel had already left to work, and only Vicentina listened to the end of the story; this time Moishele included all the details, including the mockery about the Jews being incinerated in concentration camps and the principal announcing he had been expelled.

Calmly, Vicentina told him not to worry. He should go to his room and keep studying to make up for the classes he was missing. Her words were filled with a sort of contagious security; and serene, without knowing exactly why, Moishele did what he was told. The following morning, in front of the school, on the opposite sidewalk, there she was, wearing a white lace blouse, a twirling skirt, long necklaces and a turban on her head. Sitting on the curb, she unfolded a white piece of cloth and placed a Saint George statue on it, adding some red ribbons and a bottle of *cachaça*. Next, she lit a candle.

The school was a big rectangular construction next to the sidewalk, with mansard roof and many windows facing the street, including principal Veloso's office window. Next to it, the Parish Church could be seen, with its great garden. Following her little "non-declared war," she was camped between the temple of the Christian faith, a temple of education and the principal's window.

The first person to feel bothered was Ms. Irene, the Drawing teacher. As she entered the classroom, she could see, through the window, the place where Vicentina set her "military headquarter." Very nervous, she ran to the principal's office:

"Have you seen that?"

"Seen what?"

"Open the window and you'll see."

Veloso, motivated by curiosity, quickly stood up, ran to the window and pushed its two plywood sheets. He immediately saw the esoteric arsenal across the street, guarded by a black woman, wearing clothes related to African religions.

"*Macumba*! A *macumbeira* right in front of the school, in broad daylight!" he yelled.

Ms. Irene shared Veloso's explosive revolt:

"That's absurd! I've never seen such audacity!"

Veloso said, assuming his position of "command":

"I'll put an end to that! Right now!"

He walked towards the door of the office and called someone from the secretariat next door:

"Freitas!"

Freitas, suspicious, didn't answer his first call. He only showed up after listening to Veloso non-stop screaming. Then he quietly got in, saying he was in the restroom, to avoid being chewed out by his boss. Actually, he had already seen "that," and could guess why his boss was calling him. Veloso took him close to the window and showed him the scene that was getting on his nerves.

"That's absurd," reacted the employee, subservient, using the same tone as Ms. Irene and supporting the fury seen in his boss's eyes, which reflected the image of the woman across the street.

He finally asked him:

"Get over there and tell this woman to take that *macumba* to another place!"

Freitas hesitated, but he had no option.

"Yes, Sir!" answered the trembling subordinate.

Falsely resolute, the poor employee crossed the street, getting close to the place where Vicentina remained "entrenched."

He placed himself next to her, and politely passed on the principal's message. Vicentina ignored him. She kept staring at the school, directly to the window where Veloso and Ms. Irene were lurking. The principal noticed Freita's weakness while talking to the woman; he thought he was too dull, lacking conviction. He didn't like her attitude either, she didn't even turn her head to him while he was passing on his message, acting as if no one was there.

After mechanically passing on the message, Freitas quickly returned to the office to communicate his boss that the mission had been accomplished.

"I talked to her, exactly as you told me to."

Veloso was furious:

"How? You wimpy! The *macumbeira* didn't even look at you; while you were talking, she didn't take her eyes out of here, I even think she was staring at me on purpose, she wants to push my buttons, but I won't let her!"

Veloso kept on yelling, and Ms. Irene kept repeating:

"What's the world coming to?"

"Do you want me to go there again?" suggested Freitas, "courageously" hoping he wouldn't need to cross the street again and face the "enemy."

"No, it's useless, she didn't move, I saw the way you talked to her," and he imitated the hesitant inspector. "I think you even said 'please'. Now, you stay here, otherwise you'll demoralize the establishment. I'll go there myself! If it's necessary, I'll kick all that stuff!"

Ms. Irene didn't agree; with a tone people use not to contradict someone, she said, just to the point of hiding the flattery:

"No, Sir! I'm sorry, but it makes no sense the principal of the respected Ateneu Barbosa de Oliveira having an argument in the middle of the street with a *macumbeira*. Please, stay here!"

At first, for a few minutes, Veloso strongly defended his idea of going there, in person, to take care of the eviction. But as the teacher insisted, giving him strong reasons not to expose himself, he accepted her arguments, without expressing the real relief he was feeling, pretending he was feeling bad for giving up.

He was out of the endeavor, but he needed an outlet for his wrath.

"Murilo must be involved in all that, he's never accepted losing the dispute over the school board. Mediocre as he is, a

Geography teacher who doesn't even know the measures of the *Pico da Bandeira*,[74] how can he run a school like this? It's him, I'm sure, calling on the *macumba!*"

Someone, not so down-to-earth, suggested that the Instituto Nelson Rebello, a rival school directed by a leftist, could be responsible for all the confusion. Ms. Irene suggested a technique to ignore it all:

"Let's close all front windows until she gets tired of being ignored. In any way, after the classes, we'll all leave; if she wants, she can stay there by herself with her 'thing', looking at the walls and closed windows," she stated.

Veloso agreed immediately.

"Excellent idea! If her intention is to scare us, let's pretend she doesn't exist. Everything will be back to the regular routine. Moreover, we must set an example; a place of education can't waste time with superstitions," he explained.

Outside, unconcerned about the conspiracy of the "general staff" in the principal's office, Vicentina didn't show any sign of being tired. She was going on, unshaken, with her eyes fixed on her "target," the Ateneu, as if her intention was to make it collapse, not leaving one stone upon another. Neither the principal nor any of his hasty submissive employees took time to find out if there was any tangible reason for the *despacho*, or who had ordered it, as *despachos* are always directed at someone or something. They were mobilized only by the inconvenience of the scene, and the most intimate and predictable teachers showed solidarity for the uprising.

However, Victorio, the Latin teacher, by the way the major toady, gave some precious information to the revolted workers: One of his students knew who the *macumbeira* was. And he made the bombastic revelation:

"She is a maid who works at a Jew's house, the mother of the student who was expelled!"

Suddenly, it was all clear to them. Out of her extreme

---

74 The third highest peak in Brazil, located on the border between the States of Espírito Santo and Minas Gerais.

ignorance, the little woman intended to scare the superstitious and force the board to reverse its decision, which means, to revoke the expulsion. And they started laughing out loud.

"That's ridiculous," Veloso was expressing disdain. "If it were so, I wouldn't be able to take a step here in the Ateneu without consulting a *pai de santo*. Besides, the boy deserved it, or offending a teacher's mother in the middle of the class is not enough?"

And, as a megalomaniac, he compared himself to the Almighty: "For much less than that, didn't God expel Adam from Paradise?"

Mr. Murilo risked an observation:

"He didn't have the right to defense!"

Coming from Murilo, an eternal candidate to his position, that was too hard to swallow; and the principal's reply went over the top, taking up the cudgels for Alencar, the supposed offended party.

"You say that, Murilo, because he didn't offend your mother!"

Murilo even tried to make them consider the reason for the quarreling, pointing out that all had started due to a bad joke about the Jews. Veloso thought his suggestion was ridiculous.

"Is the boy a Jew? Have you heard about any black Jew killed in a concentration camp? If you don't know, ask Gilberto, also a History teacher. It is clear the boy was not personally offended; so much so that there were two Jewish students in the classroom and they didn't care about the joke, which, at best, we can admit was sort of bad, but there was no reason for such out of proportion reaction, mainly coming from someone who has nothing to do with it. We must agree that the expulsion of the rude boy was fair, and expelled he shall remain!"

The episode, which changed the principal's mind and altered the routine in the Ateneu, started early in the morning, on a Friday, after Vicentina's arrival. The classes weren't changed until the end of the normal period, when students and employees went home. The principal, angry and squinting at the sidewalk, also left. After all, two days without classes, Saturday and Sunday, would be enough to erase the image of that woman from their minds. In the following week, the *macumbeira* would be doing her "stuff" somewhere else; at the most, he would ask the Priest from the church across the street to bless the sidewalk and all the classrooms in the Ateneu, mainly his office.

On Monday, when Veloso arrived, he noticed some teachers were waiting for him at the entrance of the building. He turned his head and got furious, a hatred compared to the one Captain Ahab felt when he saw Moby-Dick, the whale, which had already bitten his leg off.

Vicentina was still there, motionless, wearing white, next to the same *despacho* placed on the towel. Unmoved, she was only looking, or rather "targeting" at the principal's window as before. Among the ones waiting for Veloso was Priest Felix, parishioner of a nearby church, whose presence intended to join forces to chase away the bearer of evil.

It was a fuss at the Ateneu. Despite the hot weather, no one opened the front windows, trying to divert attention from the mysterious woman across the street. Priest Felix would curse non-stop against such sacrilege, an affront to his sensitivities. This was not the place for evil things or nothing of the kind! What to do? *Macumba* in broad daylight, under the hot sun, was not that unusual; and the recent Constitution of 1946 ensured the freedom of worship. "But we can't support this kind of abuse, which disturbs the operation of a house of study and revolts the sheep of my church," he yelled.

"We must call the Police," the Priest suggested.

Everyone agreed. Encouraged by the circumstantial unanimity, Veloso ran to the phone. He knew Ariosto, the Chief of Police, and described to him, with lots of details, the terrible situation and the irreparable loss due to interruptions in classes because of a fanatic and probably illiterate woman in front of his school, challenging and unapproachable. Scientifically, the Chief Officer couldn't find a relation of cause and effect between one and another, but, science apart, he could imagine Veloso's anguish. Even very important and cultured people used to keep their distance from a *despacho*. In this case, things were worse, because the person responsible was also there.

It didn't take long for the patrol to arrive. Two police officers got out of the car and lofty placed themselves in front of Vicentina; sounding as high authority, without any introduction, one of them ordered:

"Pick up those things, put out the candle and walk away!"

Vicentina didn't move a muscle. Feeling disrespected, the police officer added:

"You'd better do what you're told, for your own good, I'm not saying that again!"

The second police officer was already crouching to collect the material placed on the white towel and put out the candle. Only then, through a minimum gesture, she stared at him. He couldn't hide from her look, and, when she spoke, he became paralyzed:

"Don't you mess with the things related to Ogum!"

The police officer stood up shaking and looked at the sergeant, who has seen and heard everything. Gently moving his head, the sergeant, who was just threatening her, gave his colleague a sign. They got into the car and left promptly.

On the other side of the street, at the door of the school, there was more deception and revolt. The group followed the Police "action" from the beginning; they expected a quick outcome, the *macumbeira* would fold the towel with everything in it and leave with her tail between her legs.

Shouting, Priest Felix protested against the "surrender" of those two armed, rough men in uniform.

"This is all I need! A show of evil strength in front of so many Christians. A demoralization!"

Veloso didn't talk, and even huffed, thinking about the breach of authority. He realized the school wasn't going back to normal. The students were mocking, led by those who would do anything to avoid the boredom of the classes.

Veloso decided to hastily call all faculty and discuss what

was happening. He said he had already called the Police, but the agents were defeated by superstition and couldn't take the troublemaker away. She was still there, like a statue, staring at the Ateneu, right towards his window. He summed up the situation: a simple joke by Alencar had caused a student to overreact, and, because of that, the boy had been expelled.

Gilberto, another History teacher, requested the principal to provide more details.

"It's not necessary," Veloso answered. "What really matters is that a student offended his teacher for no reason; Alencar wasn't talking to him or to any other student, it was just a general joke."

"So, with the permission of the Board, I will present some information I gathered after listening to many students," Gilberto added.

Veloso tried to stop him, insisting it was useless to go over such unpleasant incident, which, according to him, was already under investigation and about to be solved. Gilberto didn't accept the principal's unilateralism, and got the majority support to go on.

Gilberto explained that it all happened because Alencar made a joke about the Holocaust of the Jews, a joke about the victims' bodies burned in stoves in the concentration camps. Telling a racist joke, the teacher was completely insensitive to a human drama of such magnitude. Gilberto added that this genocide had been one of the biggest crimes against humanity, and said he wouldn't have allowed any jesting or discriminatory remarks, mainly in a classroom. Moreover, any person, in this case a student, had the right, or rather, the duty, to react to what was said.

His words caused great discomfort. Automatically, all teachers turned to the author of the "joke," looking at him with reproach. Intimidated, Alencar reacted:

"What's wrong with you? Have you lost your sense of humor? The boy is the one to be blamed, I didn't even say anything about black people, why did he stick his nose in it? There are two Jewish students in the classroom; did they say anything? Nothing!"

Gilberto replicated:

"It's not only a simple racial issue; it also involves the ethics and values a teacher should convey to his students. In this case, it happened in reverse order: the one offending the ethics through an immoral joke was the teacher, and the student defended the principles which should guide a house of study such as the Ateneu."

As he set the meeting, Veloso expected a unanimity, people mitigating the issue related to the "offended" teacher. That didn't happen, and the silence and the looks on the teachers' faces made it obvious that his plan backfired.

Morally defeated, Alencar seemed unaware of how serious the situation was.

"What do you want me to do? Apologize?"

Then he used the word that would turn the situation definitely against him: "Apologize to the little 'nigger'?" He tried to rephrase, to no avail: "To the expelled student?"

The principal lowered his head, realizing a verdict was about to be given. He decided to cancel the punishment, and that Mr. Alencar should apologize to the student in the classroom. Convicted by his co-workers, Alencar went berserk.

"That humiliation? Never! This is absolutely ridiculous! How can someone even think of it? A teacher who has been working for many years, who held high positions at the Department of Education, humiliating himself in front of a black boy because of the Jews?"

Mockingly, he added, "What about the opposite? Would you apologize to a Jew because of black people? Before that, I would have requested my transfer twenty times."

His bizarre "lecture" made the Board discuss the issue. And sealed his fate. Alencar couldn't believe his eyes and ears. All of them, including the principal, were analyzing his "suggestion," which means, the possibility of requesting a transfer. The meeting has somehow turned into a "courtroom," and he was being sentenced. He looked at his colleagues and noticed they were visibly embarrassed. Feeling betrayed, he was consistent:

"Oh well, if you want my head, you'll have it! From now on, I consider myself out of the Ateneu and its faculty composed of Judas!" Irascible, he stood up and left the room without saying goodbye, going straight to the exit door.

He saw the *macumbeira* across the street, and, filled with hatred, couldn't believe she had defeated him without saying a word. Vicentina ignored him; not showing any interest, she only observed him until he got into a cab. It didn't take her long to be back on the battlefield against racial violence. At least, that single battle was over.

The relativity of time was responsible for the unexpected outcome at the Ateneu Barbosa de Oliveira. Decades ago, Alencar would probably be a slave master and Vicentina a slave. Not being able to enslave the native Brazilian population in the 16th century, the Portuguese crown decided to bring from Africa the slaves needed for the production of the high valued sugar and, later, for gold mining. The slaves were negotiated like cattle, like animals.

After the official abolition of slavery, things were not so easy for the freed slaves. Without a place to live, without any money and mainly without State support, they were relegated to total abandonment. They couldn't get a job; now free, they were victims of prejudice and racial discrimination. As a matter of survival, they disputed among themselves any type of informal and temporary work.

The urbanization of the cities gave rise to a type of work the slaves used to do. The former slave women, then their daughters, then their granddaughters, had become maids, who, until today, can be found in family houses; many of them even biological descendants of slave masters. The African culture and religion, although forbidden for a long time, had always been practiced, either through syncretism or in its pure form, and were responsible for Vicentina's resistance and victory. As almost all maids, she was an heiress of the abandonment caused by the Áurea Law.[75]

Moishele was called back to the Ateneu. The principal himself coldly apologized and he went back to his group. His stormy defense against the explicit anti-Semitism allowed Mendel to add to his paternal feeling the pride of seeing his son with open arms, facing a battle against a much stronger enemy, mainly because he had felt hurt, not concerning his ethnicity, but concerning the Jewish part of his soul.

The incident had given rise to a certain identity that, thanks to Mendel, seemed natural and unconscious — not religious, not from the synagogue neither from the sacred books nor the tradition, but, perhaps, through all of these, being dripped for a long time in his adoptive family. During the episode in the Ateneu, Moishele wasn't defending third parties; although he had formally taken up the cudgels for other people, for sentimental reasons he was also defending himself, being part of it. Culturally speaking, even being aware of the differences — equal in essence, but different in form —, he had incorporated the Hebrew two-thousand year persecution history into his own.

Vicentina was the one who, in practice, faced and defeated his opponents at the Ateneu. She knew that her determination, a result of a connection with the orishas, would allow her to run over all the cruel human obstacles, something Mendel couldn't have done. And she took that unusual battle upon herself, surprising her enemies, who only had official power and land.

It wouldn't be suitable for a Jew, a foreigner, to tackle politically influential people, as it's been during the whole history of the Diaspora. For almost two thousand years, the "chosen people" have been only unwelcomed guests in the lands they set foot, and, somehow, got used to unrestrictedly obeying his "hosts" — Czars and Emperors. For Mendel, the Ateneu's prin-

75 The law that decreed the end of slavery in Brazil

cipal was like a representative of the Czar; for Vicentina, however, he was just an ordinary man.

Mendel and Moishele were getting closer and closer, not only considering their strongly built emotional ties, but also due to mutual concern in their relationship: Mendel thought about Moishele's future and Moishele thought about Mendel's well-being.

10. Vicentina and the Chief of Police

Mendel was a goldsmith. He had learned the craft from his father and kept a small workplace in the back of his house. Moishele had taken pleasure in that art. He had learned how to make golden chains, earrings and rings. He was very creative, and used to draw models enthusiastically approved by his "master." The workplace was an industrial, commercial location, there wasn't any religious and ideological exclusiveness; they indifferently turned metal into a cross or into a star, five or six-pointed, and produced saint pendants or symbols of any religion or sect.

Believing that "times have changed," Mendel had found support in the social evolution and was able to ignore the Talmudic prohibition concerning the manufacturing of objects intended for any kind of idolatry. He was living in a great capital, no longer in the tiny and orthodox Ostrow. He worked motivated by profit, not for using the objects himself. Moishele had got many clients, including the big bosses of the infamous Animal Lottery — an illegal gambling activity in Brazil —, who really loved showing off thick golden chains, medals and bracelets. Every time he visited those "bosses" he used to take a very mixed showcase, including valuable pieces that they really enjoyed.

On one of these occasions, he faced a Police raid — something unexpected, or perhaps predictable, as he was dealing with the "bosses" of Animal Lottery. At the right moment Moishele started unfolding the velvet to show his jewelry inside the "fortress" where the bets were checked, the oppressors arrived, and were quickly attracted to his shining merchandise. Brutally, they apprehended everything, as they immediately concluded, due to the simple fact that he was a black person having such goods, that the jewelry was stolen merchandise.

Moishele uselessly tried to explain. He said he was a goldsmith, that he worked with his father and both had made the jewelry. All he got was laughter: "Father and son making jewelry, two dirty black men, that's what it is!" And they kept laughing out loud... The "fanciful" logic concerning the origin of the gold declared by the arrested boy didn't make any sense; they didn't believe Mr. Mendel was Moishele's father, and there was no way out, so the boy ended up behind bars with the "bosses." It forced Vicentina to come to his aid one more time.

It didn't take long, and a lawyer came to release the crooks. But Moishele remained arrested, and his jewelry was placed in the Chief Officer's drawer. They would try to get a confession; perhaps his untouchability for being an innocent prisoner would end soon.

When an *Umbandista* who used to work with Animal Lottery told Vicentina what had happened, she tried to talk to Mendel, but she couldn't find him. There was no time to waste; she was aware of what could happen to her son. She gathered the same "weapons" she used in the Ateneu's "battle" and ran to the door of the Police Station, without even bothering talking to any authority, as she was aware it would be useless.

The detective on duty told the jailer:

"There's a *macumbeira* right at the door! The Chief is furious!"

The news spread all over the cells.

"It's my mother!" Moishele screamed.

So, finally, everyone understood what that meant, the intention of an *Umbandista* dressed in white, sitting on a stool, in front of a white towel with a Saint George statue and a lit candle placed on it.

Accompanied by a guard, the Chief himself went down the stairs and stopped next to Vicentina. Standing up, with an authority look, he bluntly ordered:

"Get those things and get out of here!"

Vicentina gave him a threatening look. The Chief lowered his voice, but added:

"It's useless to use *macumba* to release your son; he's a jewelry thief, and he will be here for a long time!"

This time Vicentina used a different look; she looked him in the eye, but the Chief assumed the conversation was over. Showing no interest in the situation, he walked towards the stairs and started going up to his office; but after four or five steps, he fell down. Cold sweating, he placed his hand on his chest, and the guard accompanying him realized it was serious. He picked his boss up, supporting him on his shoulders, and took him to the Police car parked in front of the Station, telling the driver to quickly go to the hospital. From the car window, the Chief saw Vicentina, immovable as before. He couldn't stand the exchange of looks, and, whispering, ordered his adjunct: "Release the little 'nigger' and give all his things back!"

11. A New Look

Being under Mendel's paternal shadow for a long time, Moishele hadn't suffered any kind of racial discrimination. Now, facing the daily routine outside his house and interacting with all kinds of people, these traumatizing episodes had led him to a solitary conclusion: One day, neither Mendel nor Vicentina would be there to help him against the racist "snake," always placed under barely disguised appearances. With Mendel, he learned about the rejection against Jews, not showing it through their skins; it depended on someone pointing, or documents, or simply their own names — Isaac, Sarah, Israel... It wasn't an immediate detection. Sometimes, it could take a while for them to come up: "Are you a Jew? I've known you for so long and I didn't know..."

Historically, there has always been a kind of damaging result — bigger or smaller, depending on the time and place —, from light things, as being called sheeny or stingy, and not being allowed to enter into sophisticated clubs, up to the most dramatic things, such as being sent to concentration camps and gas chambers.

With black people, it has been different. There was no "grace period" for the rejection they suffered; it was instantaneous. Even at the drugstore, they used to be passed over by the "hierarchy" of other skins, ignoring the line.

After analyzing the racist incidents, Moishele concluded he was a helpless person, and that the best weapon against that predatory discrimination was money, lots of money, something not determined by color and respected by everyone: The more money, more respect and flattery from where there used to be only scorn. The game was reversed: The one with the fortune can be the one who discriminates; it's no longer a matter of race or color.

And he was able to find his way. He found out how to build a magical armor to be used during inevitable future confrontations, using the same gold people used to falsely accuse and arrest him. From then on, he became very dedicated to Mendel's work; he learned everything about the production of jewelry, including how to get the raw material and how to create and sell the pieces. He knew that the metal and gemstones domain, combined with his talent, would be his true and new "freedom." Mendel followed enthusiastically his professional growth, and assumed it was a natural succession. Moishele would become rich working as a jeweler; but he still had a long way to go.

Another great "discovery" was the status brought by graduation rings, indispensable for the new professionals, who were proud of their diplomas. He made many of them in his workplace, mainly using emerald green for doctors and ruby red for lawyers. He enjoyed trying each one and contemplating them on his finger, and decided he would have his own, ruby red, the most beautiful he had ever made, with a big stone that would be impossible to be ignored, bigger than the one the Chief of Police was wearing the day he arrested him. He constantly rehearsed casually placing his hand on his face, in case someone didn't call him a "doctor."[76]

Later in life, his dream came true. Moishele graduated from Law School and put the ring on his finger; he would wear it not based on vanity, but as a shield.

---

76 In Brazil, lawyers and engineers are also called "doctors."

11. MENDEL IN LOVE

Mendel turned sixty, an age that brought him the balance of time. He recalled the sexagenarian at his hometown, men with long and heavy beards, black overcoats and hats, always going or returning from the *Beit Midrash*.[77] There, where everything was a reason to be called "assimilated," he would be called a *goy*.

In Brazil, free from religious debts, he was a very different sexagenarian. He was a practitioner of Judaism with intimate enthusiasm, sustained by his faith; he used to go to the synagogue and wear a *kippah*, not as a habit, but as a spiritual necessity. He could mention a couple of transgressions, but he didn't imagine himself living without his prayers, recited since he was a kid, without the Sabbath, *Rosh Hashanah, Yom Kippur* and *Hanukkah*...[78]

But Mendel, as any human, had his weaknesses. He was proud of his looks at that age. In the morning, in front of the mirror, he not rarely whispered one of the seven morning blessings: *Baruch atah Adonai, Eloheinu melech haolam, sheh loh*

---

77 House of study of the *Torah* and the *Talmud*.

78 Meaning "dedication" in Hebrew, refers to the joyous eight-day celebration during which Jews commemorate the victory of the Maccabees over the armies of Syria in 165 B.C.E.

asani ishah — Blessed are Thou, Adonai, our God, Sovereign of the Universe, Who didn't make me a woman!

He was aware that people used to be positively surprised about his age, Faiga not so much... They didn't look as husband and wife. *Poor Faiga... she wasn't able to enjoy the happiness of maternity, which delays the wheel of time.* He felt so good that he coudn't understand the freedom granted to sexagenarian slaves, a fact brought to him by Moishele from his Brazilian History classes.

One day, a compliment concerning his looks had its consequences. Making a delivery in the jewelry shop of his old client Abraham Weiss, he was assisted by the manager, called Sylvia, and she told him that Abraham had been going through some health issues. Only at that moment, Mendel realized the beauty of that brunette on her forties, who has always been there. He had never paid any especial attention to her; it was not his style, as he was always focused on business.

She got the pieces and complimented Mendel concerning his art; he was timidly flattered. Before, he had dealt directly with Abraham, who used to pay him and didn't talk much, possibly to avoid higher prices in future deliveries.

Sylvia was familiar with the products she used to sell, and their commercial affinity ended up, as we could say, in a good chat. This was something completely new to Mendel, who used to spend his days with his friends in the synagogue, or at a Jewish club where he learned to play cards. Getting attention and admiration from a beautiful woman made him pleasantly nervous. He thought her compliments were beyond the golden pieces he brought, and it was a new sensation, although very common concerning men of his age.

Mendel had never been a womanizer. However, despite the forged barrier of living a life in which his only concern was surviving, at that moment, with sweet words coming and going between one and another glimmer, he was no longer looking at her as a manager, but as a woman. Sylvia's vibration caused him a mix of fear and desire, which he rationalized, because even being good-looking he didn't believe he was capable of attracting a much younger and so beautiful woman.

He left, allowing his imagination to fly high, only as a fantasy, trying to remember every second of that meeting consolidated through a long and glorious handshake. There was also her perfume... That farewell memory had been marked on his hand by the remains of "Fleur de Rocaille."

On the streetcar to Grajaú, his thoughts were on that sensual and gracious saleswoman from Ouvidor Street. Anesthetized, he didn't see the urban landscape in the streets, neither his ears heard the thunderous friction between the rail and the iron wheels. He was running-through every instant of delight, from the first gentle word said by the brunette who assisted him.

Sylvia, a gentile, was certainly not *kosher*. Mendel didn't know what to do; he wasn't experienced in romantic stuff, and he doubted his affection was reciprocated. The only thing he was certain was that he wanted to go back there, even without having any excuse; and it took him a while to return to his commercial responsibility and write down the new orders on his notebook.

Before arriving at his neighborhood, with much struggle, he had been able to take a few breaks from the erotic image that didn't leave his mind, and focused on his other clients, Freedman, Koogan and Levinsky, who were already scheduled. Even though he truly wished the best for Abraham, he hoped at the same time his return to health wouldn't happen too soon; then he could go to bed knowing that she would be there the next day, and her boss wouldn't.

At the entrance of his house, Mendel forgot to kiss the *Mezuzah*. In twenty years, he had religiously done it, not missing a day. But he quickly remembered, and fulfilled his obligation; and he greeted his wife with the usual arrival kiss. Faiga noticed a sort of euphoria showing on his face, but she thought it was related to a good business deal, some special sale.

During dinner, served by Vicentina, the subject was the crisis President Getúlio Vargas was going through, under attack by the journalist Carlos Lacerda. It was 1954, the beginning of August; Moishele used to follow the news, and Faiga intended to be familiar with it. She asked Mendel some questions: "What is about to come? What are people commenting in the streets, coffee shops... What is your opinion? Is any Jew involved?"

Mendel, daydreaming, gave her monosyllabic answers.

"What? Who?"

As she repeated the question, he would carelessly comment on it, being far from an accurate idea:

"Ah... This is nothing. It's only politics. Getúlio and Lacerda will come to an understanding."

"Poor Getúlio," Vicentina said, looking sad.

As always, Faiga shared her domestic misfortunes: a kitchen faucet dripping non-stop, a cockroach showing up, the phone taking too long to give a dial tone — something that would frequently happen at that time. While she was telling him her day by day problems, Mendel, distracted, illegally took refuge in that woman's magnificent smile, remembering that, a short while ago, they were talking about gold, platinum and diamonds.

Later, as it was his habit, he went to the small room where he used to pray. But in that day, God must have noticed that Mendel didn't give Him the usual attention, as he prayed quickly, skipping words and lines; most of all, he remained static, without moving his body back and forth, in the usual "rhythm" of the prayers. He had asked God to forgive him for flirting with a gentile, but he had not asked Him to take her out of his way.

All this rush praising the Creator had a reason; he wanted to go to bed early, so, during the silence, before sleeping, he could daydream of the woman who, without warning, had just entered his life. Meanwhile, lying by his side, innocent Faiga kept talking about her domestic problems, faucet, cockroach, phone... At the highest moment of his excitement, while holding the goose down pillow Faiga brought from Poland, he was arranging a delirious bouquet, putting together Sylvia's mouth, eyes and long hair, while he tried to sculp in his mind the figure of the woman who had opened the doors to a new and unsuspected universe.

Faiga unexpectedly poked him, to complain about a new leakage that had showed up after the rain. She didn't get an answer. Mendel fell asleep, or pretended he did, as he was far, far away from the marital room. Faiga postponed her rainwater drama to the morning after, and also fell asleep.

During that night, Mendel had an indecipherable dream. He dreamed he was in his hometown, Ostrow. He was walking through the Polish area, out of the conventional limits of the Jewish Street, the area of the Jews, who were the great majority in that place. From afar, he could see arms dressed in black overcoats waving at him, asking him to return. If he had returned or not, the dream didn't let him know, because, after all, dreams normally end without a conclusion, such as a movie abruptly interrupted in the middle of the story.

It was different with Sylvia. As she fell asleep, after saying the Lord's Prayer, she only thought about the commercial movement, feeling truly happy for selling a bracelet that had been in the shop for a long time. But, in the middle of the night, she woke up breathless, feeling a fuss due to a nightmare, a kind of nightmare she had never had before. Confused, she didn't know for sure if it was a nightmare or an indefinable type of disturbing dream: A smiling man showed up in front of her, totally naked; and, as if the enormity of the dreamy sin wasn't enough, she was shocked when she saw his penis didn't have the foreskin. *Have I just had a libidinous dream with a Jew?* she reprimanded herself.

Terribly ashamed, she had to tell it all to her confessor in the following Sunday Mass. How come a former novice — almost a nun, who hadn't made the vows because her father got sick and she had to work and take care of him — could have had such a dream?

The confessor attentively listened, as she was telling him about her appalling night "adventure." He didn't blame her, he had frequently heard about such dreams in his confessional. He had only paid closer attention to the foreskin detail, but he reassured her explaining that "the person in your dream is not necessarily a Jew; any Christian man can have a surgery for Phimosis and remove that little wrinkle."

Sylvia, happy with his explanation, added some more facts concerning her work, because she had to "push" a piece that wouldn't sell to a client, following her boss's guidance. She got general absolution and, relieved, she received communion.

The next morning, during breakfast, Mendel patiently listened to Faiga's report about the leakage and its damages. He didn't care about the loss, and he promised her he would ask Mister Cardoso, the handyman, to check the roof tiles. As he left, he was even more lucid about his pre-romantic experience, and kept harping on the same string, considering himself a fool and pretentious man: *I'm making a mess out of the things. She enjoyed my work as a goldsmith; and my desire distorted her admiration.* He mentally punished himself: *Am I irresponsible enough to imagine an extra-marital affair?* Far more serious was the fact that the woman responsible for such a fantasy had a golden cross on her chest, which he made himself.

Considering an affair, he would be facing elements that he could not manipulate as gold: his religion, his marriage, his community, a very Christian girlfriend. He shivered, as he imagined that an affair could shake his calm and endogamous Yiddish marriage; he remembered the wedding ceremony, during which he stepped on and shattered a crystal glass, symbolizing a union that could only be broken when all the pieces were back together.

An adventure... It was is all he needed at this point of his life! But tomorrow is another day... He kept that sentence in mind to reaffirm his decision to resist at all costs. On the other hand, however, the persevering ambiguity of his people brought him the foretaste of paradisiacal compensations, which he had never had or hoped. *After all, didn't King Solomon have a thousand wives? Of all ethnicities?*

After a long and tempting digression, Mendel finally assumed the "danger" was gone; he even relied on another biblical saying, which reveals what would happen to those who couldn't resist such whim: the end of Samson in Delilah's hands. Devoid of second intentions, as he surely believed, he decided to go back to the jewelry shop to deliver new earrings and chains. He still had some time concerning his deadline, but, as he had anticipated other deliveries, he could also anticipate Abraham's, *a purely commercial measure, with nothing to do with her,* he repeated to himself, with little conviction. He would deliver the goods, get the payment and that would be all! He wouldn't allow the conversation to get more intimate, on either side. He heard about a Jew friend who got involved with a *shiksa*[79] and got into a lot of trouble; he ended up leaving his family, and when he died he was buried in a Christian cemetery.

In the synagogue, he had asked about Abraham; he heard he was still in the hospital due to a surgery. He avoided associating this fact to a longer absence of his friend and client, which meant that Sylvia would be available to freely assist him at any time; he couldn't even think of inviting her for coffee. He would prove to himself that their first meeting had simply been a meeting between two people with similar professional ideas — he, a manufacturer, she, an experienced jewelry saleswoman —, nothing more. It wouldn't make any difference if from then on he needed to make deals with her or with Abraham. They would only talk about the pieces, the prices, the deadlines and so on.

Cautious, he would avoid looking at her eyes, he would talk to her looking at her mouth, *not the mouth, no! It's too beautiful!* He gave up. He would talk to her looking at her nose, but then he remembered: *No, not the nose. She's got a gorgeous Greek nose.* He decided he should be strong; he would look at whatever pleased him, hair, eyes, nose, hands... It didn't matter, she was a gentile, an insurmountable obstacle to any emotional progress, even more serious than his marital status.

Sticking to this preconceived plan, he walked up Uru-

---

79 Derogatory Yiddish word meaning "non-Jewish girl," especially one who is attractive and young. In South America, it can also mean "maid."

guaiana Street, turned on Ouvidor Street and saw the shop. *She is right there. I'll act naturally, I'll treat her as an ordinary client, I won't be influenced by her voice, neither her eyes, nor her long hair...* He couldn't understand why his heart was beating so fast, it had never happened when he was about to meet Abraham. He had a passion fruit juice to calm him down. He simply couldn't understand, or didn't want to, why he was so nervous concerning a strictly commercial visit.

Sylvia warmly welcomed him; her wide smile was not the usual one she would give her clients, much less her suppliers. If any look was showing enchantment, it wasn't his, it was hers. After a long handshake, Mendel deleted all he had "rehearsed." Shyly, he started the conversation:

"I brought some golden chains Abraham ordered some time ago." He omitted the real deadline in order to avoid "misunderstandings" concerning the true reason of his visit.

"They're very beautiful," Sylvia exclaimed, examining the pieces.

Mendel tried to look indifferent.

"As everything you make," she added, pointing at the pieces displayed in the shop window.

Mendel's eyes sparkled; his biggest weakness was related to his artistic vanity.

"Do you know which pieces were made by me?" he asked, crazy to hear compliments from the woman who could understand his art.

Sylvia took a solitaire ring which was exposed and put on her finger.

"I know this ring is yours, so delicate... An arch well done, a spotless diamond combined with yellow gold. I can imagine how delicate the moment of placing the stone is, so subtle..."

It's known that the state of love can turn any mature man into the silliest creature alive; this had never happened to Mendel, and it wasn't expected to happen, as he has always lived, not under orthodox rules, but respecting the habits and ethical conventions of the Jewish society. As a jeweller, he had had fleeting commercial contacts with very beautiful women, but he had never felt weak at the knees until that moment.

He appropriately thanked her, impulsively taking advantage of the situation to show that, not being able to resist, he slipped away from a feeling he considered dominated. He took her hand and stared at the solitaire. *Is she, without realizing, trying to tell me something by putting this ring?* Sounding as a teenager, he whispered:

"The most beautiful jewel here is you..."

Sylvia didn't laugh as she heard an unexpected comment from a much older man. Mendel was exhaling sweat and sincerity through all his pores, and the lady's reddish face denounced she wasn't indifferent to the flattery; he knew she had listened to his meaningful words. She placed her other hand on his, and told him:

"Mendel..."

The "mister" was gone, the age difference wouldn't be a problem anymore. Unlikely? Not so much. If Dr. Jekyll was able to turn himself into Mr. Hide, why wouldn't Mendel suddenly turn into a clumsy, but passionate Don Juan? His knees stopped shaking, but he felt as an offender of all laws mentioned in the books at the synagogue.

He felt like running away. The providential arrival of an old client reestablished normality. Mendel took the opportunity and discreetly said goodbye:

"I'll come back another day to check if Abraham liked the chains. If you see him, please send him a hug."

From Ouvidor Street, walking fast, he reached Rio Branco Avenue and kept walking with no destination. He felt like a naughty boy. He was under the impression that all the bystanders, Jewish or non-Jewish, were staring at him. He put his *Kippah* in his pocket. In his mind, scattered aerial images were spinning around, as in a Chagall's painting, close or distant things, prohibitions and recurring guilt associated with the moment: his wife Faiga, the Rabbi, the ones who attended the synagogue and even the Christian procession during the Holy Friday in Ostrow.

He stopped at a pub, and, for the first time in his life, he had a draft beer. Only after the second glass, he was able to reasonably think straight. He felt good for being able to call the attention of such a beautiful woman, much younger, a treasure. *But what should I do with this feeling?* Only thinking about the next step made him panic, before his imagination would go from a simple handshake to an imaginary and sequential embrace. The fact that she was a Christian was no obstacle. Mendel, beforehand, justified his thoughts through a bunch of "reasons," created by his own will.

I won't marry her, I won't have kids. Faiga has no reason to complain, we've been together for many years and she never lacked anything; according to the Jewish law, the husband can even repudiate an infertile wife... Besides, everything will remain the same; I'll be very careful, she'll never know about the other woman. I know her quite well, even if she found it out, she would understand and say nothing. Jewish women are different from the Latinas; all they care about is the kids. We don't have kids, and she is the infertile one; a Jewess without children becomes almost indifferent to this fidelity stuff, she has no self-esteem, she feels way too inferior to complain. If she suspects something, she will pretend she didn't see it. This was, at the moment, the way he saw things.

But what about the *Torah*? And the *Talmud*? How could he face the sacred obligations? He insisted on the biblical saying: *Solomon, the wisest of all kings, had a thousand wives!* He wouldn't repeat the Nazi dogma, which punished the minimum contact between a Jew and an Aryan woman. As he married Faiga, he had already paid his tribute to his people's customs. A secular Jew dating a Christian, if uncovered, would cause, of course, a lot of gossip and malicious comments in the community, mainly among the ladies who used to meet every evening to play cards: "Mendel was seen with a *shiksa*, and it's not the first time!"

Naturally, they would show solidarity to the cheated wife: "Poor Faiga, at home taking care of her domestic chores and her husband downtown having fun with another woman." No doubt, the soothsayers of chaos would be around: "Suddenly, a pregnant woman will show up at her door saying Mendel is the baby's father." And another: "It will be a shame, the neighbors seeing all that! And how would he go to the synagogue on *Yom Kippur*? Everyone will know why he's asking for forgiveness."

It was all speculation, due to his anxiety. He calmed himself through different mental mechanisms: *I'm sure nothing like that will happen; many men from the synagogue have affairs, I suspect many of them keep a paramour in the suburb since they started to sell products in installments.*

As he recovered his self-control, he started to walk calmly and took the streetcar home. As before, he ignored the bumps, and daydreamed about what had happened; he even considered it the best day of his life. *So, that's what love is all about.* He compared meeting Sylvia to the couples' insipid dates on the immigration ship, such as his: *That was not love; on board together for so many days, we got used to each other; or maybe it was a different kind of love, a result of the fear of facing the unknown alone. How many couples got married based on that?*

He mentally discarded all the "ifs," and gave himself a safe-conduct to go back to the jewelry shop the next day. He didn't have any deliver, but it didn't matter; he no longer needed an excuse. He arrived home feeling bewildered, and it took him some time to re-adapt to the domestic environment.

Faiga asked him if he had lost his *kippah*. Embarrassed, he took it off his pocket and blamed the heavy wind for not wearing it. Next, his wife asked him what he had done concerning the persistent roof infiltration. Patiently, Mendel didn't get upset for being abruptly transported from Eden to a corner of the living room, where an aluminum bucket was under the persistent dripping. He promised her, once again, he would call someone to fix it soon. Then he went to the shower and kept dreaming.

In bed, he was flying over the clouds; and as usual was interrupted by Faiga, who poked him to complain about the fridge that wasn't working well. Mendel grunted and fell asleep, smiling. However, he dreamed of Abraham, who was back in the jewelry shop, recovered and vigilant, not allowing him to approach his pupil. He woke up relieved, and went back to sleep after asking God for Abraham's complete recovery, even if took some time… emphasizing that the most important thing was his friend's good health. It was in God's hands to decide the day he would return to work.

The next day, during breakfast, Mendel, nonchalantly, talked about a new project: "I feel like buying a new car. What do you say? The old Ford is falling to pieces."

"I was thinking about that, you know?" Faiga agreed, innocently complying with her husband's Machiavellian plan. He already could romantically imagine himself as a medieval knight, "driving" his new "four-wheel horse" with a beautiful, delighted damsel by his side, enjoying the ride. Actually, he was deceiving his wife.

"Moishele will be able to drive Faiga to her more distant friends' houses, and the old car cannot do it," Mendel obliquely reinforced the purchase plan; and his naive wife was touched by his project of buying her a new car.

He also said he was counting on Moishele to drive on sanctified days, since as a Jew he couldn't do it. He thought that as a passenger, not driving, he would get around the Talmudic prohibition of any locomotion in which he wouldn't use his own feet, an inappropriate use of the "Brazilian smart way," concerning the strictness of the sacred holidays. Faiga thought this modern interpretation of the Scriptures was quite strange, but she didn't cast doubt on it.

Vicentina was the only one who noticed Mendel had changed, that he was hiding something; but she didn't seem to be worried about it.

Freudian knowledge must have explained it somewhere: All adulterers are necessarily Machiavellian and liars. In short: Pretending he was purchasing a new car to offer more comfort to his family, what Mendel really had in mind was having romantic dates in places where his current car couldn't take him, as it was emitting smoke and a strong smell of gasoline inside and out.

He wasn't really sure about the acquisition, but, anyhow, almost everyone got involved in the new automobile industry wave; in a period of high inflation, certain brands were considered a good investment. In addition, "youth was not a time of life; it was a state of mind" — he resorted once again to an overused saying, already thinking about his favorite model. He wanted to have more time and pleasure while meeting Sylvia, eliminating the well-behaved and noisy streetcar rides. Replacing his slow car, which stopped many times on the way, they would be back home at their usual time, avoiding the typical question: "What happened? Why have you arrived late?"

There was no doubt in his mind it would be a lawbreaker romance, an affair that would meet the laws of love probability. Mendel was a married man, a non-orthodox Jew, but a good follower of the religious traditions and obligations. He was one of those who would daily pray with his *tallit* and *tefillin*,[80] and his group was the group from the synagogue. Only the fact of not having a child would go against the underlying precepts of a Hebrew home, but Mendel had already accepted that, and Moishele's casual arrival had somehow filled this gap.

In his hometown, a simple and fleeting relationship with a Christian Polish woman would become a subject in the community and arise thousands of warnings from parents, grandparents, any relative on Earth. In Poland, you couldn't be too careful; in each mass, the ancient Christianism fostered an anti-Semitic religious stigma. In the villages, a Jew setting foot in a Christian church, for any reason, would equal a mortal sin.

The shock between the two religions was inevitable. He knew that Sylvia's family was Roman Christian, all very devoted.

---

80 Hebrew for phylacteries (from Ancient Greek, meaning "to guard, protect"), a set of small black leather boxes containing scrolls of parchment inscribed with verses from the *Torah*, which are worn by observant Jews during weekday morning prayers.

They would go to church every Sunday, follow all the processions and take part in the charity fairs, offering gifts and working at some stalls; they wouldn't miss the church benefit bingo. At home, a picture of the Last Supper on the wall left no doubt about the prevailing faith.

At odds with himself, Mendel carefully planned his next love steps. At the beginning, he would spare her more "daring" gestures of affection, in order to avoid misunderstandings following a long tight embrace or a goodbye kiss; he would hide his true intentions, or his suppressed desire, to guarantee none of his gestures would suggest any kind of commitment, something that terrified him. Above all, he would never say "I love you!"

If she said it, he would be quiet, instead of automatically answer: "Me too!"

Silly man... Naive and fearful, he thought he could control the uncontrollable.

12. D-Day

Since that enchanted day in Abraham's jewelry shop, under the pretext of delivering pieces, the sexagenarian Mendel started thinking and acting as any incipient man in love. Few are the known prisoners of passion who weren't splashed by the ridiculous, who wouldn't step up in direct proportion to their age, like a faun hit by Cupid's arrow. Mendel didn't know a thing about Julius Caesar, he never heard the story of the Roman Emperor who crossed the Rubicon River — a sign of insurrection defined by a Senate law, created to prevent their own generals from advancing on Rome. Saying "*Alea jacta est*,"[81] Julius Caesar broke the rule and seized the power. Mendel could not refer himself to the historic citation, but, considering time, space and goals, he also crossed his prosaic Rubicon. And, cumulatively, he invaded his private "Normandy" the moment he decided to conquer something which, for him, was more pleasurable than an empire, more powerful than any military strategy.

He planned a "casual" meeting with Sylvia out of the commercial establishment. One day, from a distance, he observed her as she closed up shop and followed her towards the streetcar stop. Walking on the parallel street, he got his happy "coincidence": Sylvia arrived and he was there, pretending to read the

---

81 From Latin: "The die is cast."

newspaper. It was the meeting, with no return, of a son of the *Torah* and a beautiful Roman Christian, almost a devotee.

When he saw her, he pretended to be surprised. He greeted her, folding the newspaper: "What a coincidence!"

Genuinely surprised, Sylvia naturally answered:

"I take this streetcar every day, but I've never seen you."

He felt this "seen you" as a heavenly nectar. If she had chosen to say "Mister," he would give up right there, would keep reading the newspaper, make up any excuse, miss the streetcar... and a much desired and forbidden love story. As the streetcar started moving, a love story started, with all the generic ingredients of Romeo and Juliet, not in a square in Verona, but in Largo de São Francisco,[82] both uncomfortably sitting on a streetcar called "17", heading to Lins de Vasconcelos.[83]

Ordinary love stories grow in every corner of the Earth, in different forms and variable contexts; and also family dramas, for religious reasons or not. Forbidden love affairs feed piles of screenplays and literary works. Who hasn't heard similar stories, or has even lived one of them with family or friends? Girls in love with boys who don't enjoy working, classical and common examples of family opposition: a bum Romeo and a challenging Juliet are never lacking in any district. Their story was somewhat like that, but under the form of a rough biblical clash — involving the Old and the New Testament —, that was ready to bloom under the unromantic verses in the ads of Rhum Creosotado,[84] in which the "neat good-looking type" was saved from bronchitis by the powerful syrup.

If they had visited any cheap fortune-teller in the suburb, she would have known "that streetcar" would never arrive at a "safe haven." Mendel should know he was "asking for trouble;"

---

82 A famous square in downtown Rio de Janeiro.
83 District in the North region of Rio de Janeiro.
84 Name of an old Brazilian syrup used for respiratory diseases which used poems in its ads.

he should have noticed "their saints didn't match,"[85] literally, since there are no saints in Judaism.

They rode together, sitting side-by-side. Mendel was discreetly monitoring the journey; there could be a friend around, as, at each stop, more people were boarding the streetcar. If it were a Jew, or mainly a Jewess, a simple chat with a *shiksa* would be the subject of choice during the next day ladies' card game; at night, he would be mocked by the poker players in the house of Israel Wrotslawsky, a big fabric wholesaler from Senhor dos Passos Street. Mendel was particularly afraid of being seen by his neighbor Moyses Kestenberg, a Jewish scholar of the *Torah*, who wouldn't accept any transgression concerning the sacred books, habits and traditions. Neither should they be the target of the comments from ordinary passengers. He removed his *kippah* — for Mendel, a rather significant gesture, meaning much more than the simple act of putting a folded little piece of cloth in his pocket.

The use of a *kippah* is a sign of respect and reverence to the Creator. A few Jews walk around with the skullcap on their heads on a daily basis, and the ones who wear it feel as disobedient sons when they are without it. Mendel's gesture clearly demonstrated the power of the temptation that had dominated him — religion was no longer a priority. And, if faith removed mountains, it wouldn't come as a surprise that eroticism would remove faith itself. Perceptions and convictions accumulated throughout a whole existence can fade away cracked by passion in a few symbolic seconds, the time required, for example, to hide the round cloth a Jew puts on his head to remind him that "Someone" up there is protecting him; but also watching him...

Mendel tried to hide his obvious restiveness, his lack of self-confidence. He would do anything for a glass of draft beer. He wasn't sure about anything, once again insecure for having a young woman within reach. He had a relapse, and carefully analyzed every sentence, every word: *And if it's all about being*

---

85 A Brazilian idiomatic expression, "saints that match" would mean the couple hit it off straightaway.

nice to older people? Or an exclusively professional admiration concerning my pieces? He feared rejection, felt as a "ridiculous old man" flirting with a girl who could be his daughter; and decided not to go forward. He thought about taking off his wedding ring, but gave up; it would be a useless lie, as he hadn't done it before.

His newly aroused voluptuousness left no room for thinking about his wife. Transgressors, of any type or degree, plead their own cases concerning facts, feelings and circumstances. *The type of fidelity he owned Faiga wouldn't be affected,* he thought. His innocuous marriage routine and a possible affair were completely separated realities; they could live together, each one in its own dimension. Faiga would keep blessing the Sabbath candles and managing the domestic problems, no visible change would be able to disrupt their lives.

Armed with this arsenal of justifications, Mendel turned off, one by one, all the warning signs which were blocking his trajectory towards this love that had crossed his way due to a friend's surgery. Mendel, the Polish Jew, had left Ostrow — his hometown, which represented poverty and persecution — dreaming of peace and fortune. In Brazil, he was able to find what he was looking for. However, the trip that truly had changed his life lasted an hour, if so; and it hadn't been on a transatlantic, it took place on a prosaic streetcar leaving from Largo de São Francisco, sitting next to Sylvia.

Formally, the first words spoken were related to her boss's health:

"How is Abraham doing?" Mendel asked.

"He's getting better, but he's still very weak."

Showing theatrical compassion, Mendel, always slyly specific, wanted to get more information about the return of her boss to work — his main concern, followed by a genuine desire for Abraham to get well. The longer he took to recover, the more opportunities he would have to be with Sylvia without "inspection."

Sylvia's answer was, therefore, "encouraging":

"It's impossible to know, the doctors want him to rest."

Mendel focused, then, on the "business agenda":

"How are the sales?"

Nervous about this kind of "first time," he tried to make her speak, so he would be able to slowly recover his heart rate, a feeling similar to taking homeopathic tablets, which, normally, take long to take effect.

"They dropped a little, but I believe they will get better at the end of the year; the best men clients wait for Christmas to please their wives and secret lovers. Some don't even bother disguising, they buy two pieces which are exactly the same... And even ask me to write their names on the cards."

Mendel, ironically, added:

"The big risk is changing cases while delivering them."

"I've never thought of it," Sylvia laughed, imagining the husband's ordeal while explaining to his wife the gift received as a mistake.

Mendel kept on the business "camouflage," trying to gain time. As soon as the topic "purchase and sale" was over, he would be able to find a gap to get more intimate.

"What's been helping the jewelry business is that many people are buying jewelry as an investment, due to the high inflation which keeps going up," he commented.

Sylvia agreed, and added:

"Not to mention the price of gold, which increases at all times; Abraham constantly calls to check the prices... and gets really angry..."

Finally, a baby, who was on the lap of a woman sitting in front of them, changed the course of the conversation.

"Mendel, do you have kids?"

"No, unfortunately, my wife wasn't able to get pregnant. But I've got a foster child, a boy, my maid's son, who came to my house as a baby. He's now 17."

Mendel felt comfortable to ask her a similar question:

"What about you? Have you ever been married?"

Sylvia was pleased with his question, as someone

who's looking for an opportunity to vent and find someone to listen.

"It's a long story, I didn't get married, but I was close."

Mendel encouraged her to talk about it:

"Of course, you, such a beautiful lady, must have had lots of suitors."

"No, it's not that... I mean I interrupted a novitiate, the preparatory period before becoming a nun. The nuns are married to Jesus Christ."

"And why did you give up?"

"Because my father got really sick and wasn't able to work anymore; as an only child, I had to give up. I'd already met Abraham, I used to go to his jewelry shop to pay the installments. Aware of our situation, and, by coincidence, in need of someone to work in the shop, he ended up inviting me to be a saleswoman; little by little, I learned about the business."

Mendel courted her in his own way:

"It was the best business of his life..."

Sylvia added, joking:

"I believe that what he really considered was the fact that my mother never delayed the installments!"

The former attentive Mendel took the opportunity to relax completely:

"He just needed to take a look at your mother's payment book... He didn't even bother asking for references."

The streetcar passed in front of a movie theater, and the title of the movie, "Love is a Many-Splendored Thing," called her attention.

"I really want to watch this movie. I used to go to the movies with my mother all the time; now, due to my father's illness, she barely leaves home."

Mendel thought it was a great opportunity to say something like "if you want, I can take you...", but he restrained himself. It wouldn't be easy to resist, at least for the time being, the temptation of getting into a dark room with that fascinating woman, touching her hair and listening to her whispers about the romantic movie. He wasn't psychologically prepared yet to have this non-*kosher* portion of heaven. He took a deep breath and simply observed the movement of the streetcar through the streets and avenues, stifling the words which were ready to be said.

He wasn't a daring man. Ambiguous? No doubt. He simply "wanted, without wanting"; or would it be "not wanting, wanting?" He was fooling himself, postponing the unavoidable moment he would gluttonously touch any part of that desirable *shiksa*'s body and light the flame of a double betrayal: Cheating his wife and the synagogue. It would be less serious if instead of Christian Sylvia were Jewish like him.

They arrived in Grajaú, his stop. A handshake, which started much before the stop, was followed by an expected question:

"Are you taking the streetcar tomorrow at the same time?"

Sylvia answered, smiling:

"Always..."

Mendel was wandering, ignoring everything around him; his mental activity was limited to recalling pleasant moments from that short trip. He was simply walking, not paying any attention to the bystanders or cars, remaining indifferent to the commercial results of the day. In his heart, there was no place for material things, much less important at that time. He only had thoughts about Abraham's beautiful manager, who was riding the streetcar home.

He was balancing the religion's precepts again. Reviewing, not so accurately, several Talmudic prohibitions, he didn't find anything that would condemn the strict pleasure of physical contact with a woman, independently of her faith — at least not anything so restrictive such as eating pork. And he couldn't remember anything more pleasant than simply being next to her, not even comparing it to the days he had spent with his poor fiancée, during his youth, in Ostrow.

Mendel had finally understood how poets felt, talking

about the moon and the stars. *They're so right!* On his own, for lyrical effect, he compared the old streetcar to the celestial bodies; and reconsidered his opinion about love verses: They were not as silly as he had thought before. He was surprised that he hadn't heard about any romantic poet among the great Jewish writers. There were the Russians, but their verses were all related to the exaltation of the communist revolution.

Disregarding his routine, it had taken him some time to realize that the following day would be a Friday; normal business hours extended into the Sabbath, which started around 6 p.m. He would have to go home earlier in obedience to the day of rest, he wasn't allowed to ride a car or streetcar after the first star appeared in the sky. He wouldn't be able to see Sylvia until the following week.

Earlier, on Friday, he would have to go to a grocery shop on Santana Street to buy a *challah* and horseradish for the *gefilte fish* that made Faiga proud. Challenging, she would boast around saying she cooked the best fish ball of all, either in Brazil or in her hometown, just as she criticized a well-known specialist in Jewish food: "Frida Losinsky's *gefilte fish* takes too much sugar." In addition, the quality of the fish Faiga was using had improved a lot since she started going to the street fair with Vicentina.

Mendel felt bad. He had almost forgotten the sacred rest because of a simple and sinful ride on streetcar 17. When he arrived home, he found a worried Faiga, saying she needed to talk to him. Of course, she couldn't talk about something that didn't exist out of the borders of his desire; even so, he was kind of shocked, his emotion was not considering his brain information telling him he had nothing to fear.

Faiga pointed her finger, not at him, but at the ceiling, and said, in her most serious tone:

"Look at the mess Mister Cardoso did, right there! The leakage is worse than before, it was a waste of money!"

Only at this point Mendel's heart could connect to his brain, and he felt relieved, getting rid of the suppressed tension he was keeping up to that moment, concerning his imaginary sensation of being caught for something he hasn't even done. Falsely, he agreed with his wife, and also blew up at poor Mister Cardoso.

"You're right, Faiga! That dirty man charged a fortune and it's all the same mess, tomorrow I'll talk to him!"

After being abruptly taken out of a sensual Nirvana to deal with persistent raindrops and lousy services, Mendel, already recovered, locked himself in the bedroom and started "listening to the stars" again. He went to the shower, and Faiga was intrigued to hear him humming, for the first time, "*Bei Mir Bist Du Shein*" (To me you are beautiful).

He had dinner and went to bed as he was returning to the clouds, that means, being on that elusive streetcar. He was morally a bigamist: He had a woman in his mind and another materially next to him, in his marital bed.

Mendel felt sorry for Faiga. He looked at her, so naive, sound asleep, perhaps dreaming of her leakages and her noisy TV. He compared the image in front of him to Sylvia's silhouette, and convinced himself that he was getting a "good deal."

I'll make it up to Faiga, he repeated, adding a bit more to what has already been established: He would spend more time with her, would constantly visit friends with her, they would eat out, he would buy a new TV etc., in addition to other typical marriage activities, without arguments.

He implemented the new domestic system, devoting the weekends to his family. There had been a while since they visited Quinta da Boa Vista, with its National Museum and amusement park. Moishele was no longer a kid, and, because of that, he thought at first the idea was very strange; but, after a while, he got excited. Mendel made sure Vicentina would go with them.

Faiga and Moishele were teasing each other: Who would be brave enough to ride the Ferris wheel? And the roller coaster? Machiavellian Mendel observed the good results of his strategy. He didn't take sides concerning the "argument," saying the only risk he would take was eating non-*kosher* popcorn.

They spent Sunday covered in illusion, which was registered by a pinhole photograph. Having fun with them fulfilled Mendel's necessity of bribing his own conscience, the result of a private and improvised sense of justice demanding compensation for a precocious and just outlined guilt. From that moment on, he would eventually organize other leisure activities in order to satisfy his lawbreaker ego; he even encouraged his wife to search for theater plays. He would need to, somehow, rearrange his married life: Faiga would keep the honors of Sabbath and the Sunday joys; and he would keep his enchanted daily rides back home accompanied by a beautiful woman.

Finally, on Monday, Mendel would be able to meet Sylvia with a bit more intimacy. He heard Abraham was getting better and would soon return to work, meaning they wouldn't be so comfortable in the jewelry shop. The streetcar oasis was all they could count on.

"I missed you on Friday, Mendel," Sylvia said, feeding his vanity, as he was expecting to hear those exact words.

"I missed you too, but I forgot to tell you that, on Fridays, the Sabbath starts in the late afternoon. After a certain time, due to religious reasons, the Jews are not allowed to work or do anything which disrupts the day of rest."

"Is it forbidden to ride the streetcar during the Sabbath?"

"The religion, according to our sages, allows us to walk on foot; public transportation isn't allowed, which of course it's not always possible."

"Oh well; anyway, we've got Mondays, Tuesdays, Wednesdays and Thursdays," Sylvia added, counting the days on her fingers.

She placed her hand in Mendel's hand; he did the same, as they had already rehearsed the other day. During the ride, bouncing up and down, the dating was "official." Mendel joked, pointing at the already known ad:

"I thank the Rhum Creosotado!"

"For what?"

"The neat good-looking type sitting next to me."

Sylvia laughed out loud, and wittily answered:

"Well, you should know I've never, in my whole life, taken this Rhum stuff."

The joke with the syrup resulted in a first, brief kiss Mendel gave her on the cheek, repeated on the next day, and during weeks, until he was able to acquire the naturalness and reactions of an obstinate adulterer, a gift that can only be acquired through practice.

Mendel arrived home feeling as a delinquent, his heart beating as fast as the heart of a fugitive. As a good psychologist, and knowing his wife's weaknesses, he took the habit of bringing her sweets, which fanned Faiga's gluttony and curiosity every time she looked at the little pack he was carrying. While his wife was unwrapping and trying the candies, Mendel evaded telling her "how his day was," avoiding contradictions or stuttering. He would go straight to the shower.

As time went by, more confident, he thought these minor compensations were no longer necessary. It is a fact that the love escalation has no return, even for a beginner. As the first step was taken, conventionally, soon the second will come, and will go on respectively up to infinite... After that ardent handshake — a "magnitude one" infidelity, almost nothing on the Richter Scale of cheating —, whenever he sexually thought about his muse, even in public places, Mendel used the *Jewish Tribune* to make sure bystanders wouldn't notice his surprising and not so shy erection. This inconvenience was something unusual, almost a miracle concerning his age, which could only be controlled when Mendel mentally replaced Sylvia's imaginary nudity by the also imaginary face of Isaac Singer, a bearded Rabbi from his hometown.

Before falling asleep, a moment to guess what was to come, Mendel used to plan the shortest way towards his "beloved Sylvia" — that's how he called her in his thoughts. In bed next to him, as the leakage problem was already solved, Faiga worried about the dress she would wear the next day, during a meeting of the women's committee to raise money for the young State of Israel.

Very carefully, with the utmost secrecy, Mendel was planning to take Sylvia to the movies, to watch "Love is a Many-Splendored Thing." No doubts, during the movie, the plot of that torrid romance would provide the moment and emotion for a tight embrace, and, who knows, even a substantial kiss motioned by the romantic soundtrack during the scenes between the charming American and the beautiful oriental doctor. He had already seen of the movie — impassive, with his wife —, and was aware of its sentimental load. He had kept in mind it was mandatory to watch it again, this time with Sylvia, because with Faiga it had been a waste.

He bought the tickets and waited for her in front of the theater. Their seats were in the last row, as planned by Mendel to avoid attention towards and older man and such young woman — at that time, there were ushers in the movies using flashlights. Not to mention the fact that they would be embarrassed by someone sitting right behind them.

Mendel had already observed how teens used to behave. During the first half of the movie, he only held her hand. Then, carefully, he embraced her. And kept the embrace all through the second half. Every time he tried to touch her face with his own, he found some delicate resistance; but he was aware he had a trump card. As the movie was ending, the drama brought tears to her eyes. She was vulnerable…

He didn't want to take risks, so he would wait for the last scene, in which William Holden's ghost showed up from the top of a hill to say goodbye to Jennifer Jones, to the sound of "Love is a Many-Splendored Thing." Mendel was proving to be a good and empirical connoisseur of the female soul…

This time, there was no resistance. They kissed until the lights were turned on, motivated by the most exhilarating background music on the face of the Earth. The golden cross on her chest barely touched the Star of David on his.

At home, the spontaneous excuse for arriving late was the same: traffic jam. By getting home at different times, Mendel had just created a new daily schedule, and Faiga, who didn't even have plumbing or pluvial problems to talk about, did not detect the obvious happiness on his face. His affability towards his wife was directly proportional to his anxiety.

He was constantly looking forward to the nights with Sylvia, and spontaneously counting the hours until the moment she would show up, shining, at their meeting point; but as he saw her the following day, he missed her usual smile, he noticed she was different. Was it caution, or anything related to the stolen kiss?

"Do you regret anything?"

"No... Why?"

"Something is bothering you..."

"You're right! I'm worried about Priest Felix."

"Why? I'm not worried about Rabbi Meyer."

"In your religion, it's different."

"How different?"

"To be acquitted of my sins, I must confess every Sunday. I confess and commune."

Mendel was moved by Sylvia's religious enthusiasm, but couldn't resist the Jewish habit of minimizing concerns.

"You're luckier than me," he said.

"Why?"

"Because you can be acquitted every Sunday; the Jews are only acquitted once a year, in the Day of Atonement."

"I know, on *Yom Kippur*. Abraham doesn't open the shop that day, and he fasts all day. Do you fast too?"

Mendel hesitated to answer.

"Yes, I mean, so-so..."

"So-so? What do you mean?"

"I can't bear not having breakfast."

"And don't you eat anything?"

"Almost nothing... just a small piece of black bread."

"I know, I've already tasted it; now and then, Abraham brings it to the shop."

"In the confessional, do you have to say that we went to the movies?"

"Of course!"

"Including all details?"

"Yes… to be meaningful."

"And what if the Priest considers it a sin?"

Sylvia, a bit embarrassed, explained:

"If it's a small sin, he'll ask me to pray the Lord's Prayer three times; I'll only know on Sunday, during mass."

On Monday, Mendel wanted to know about Sylvia's penitence.

"Ten Lord's Prayer and ten Hail Mary," she said, whining.

"That's absurd! All because of a kiss? Haven't you explained to the Priest it was just a simple one?"

"It doesn't make any difference, the sin is the same. It increased a lot due to another thing."

"What thing?"

"I confessed I had kissed a Jew."

His Jewish roots made him mock her, using a business tone.

"In this case, we can kiss ten, twenty times, and it will be the same."

Sylvia decided that the best solution would be reducing the number of confessions. Her parents would find it strange, but she would come up with any excuse. Mendel made a subtle and malicious question that made her laugh:

"Tell me something, have you, once, received a great penitence? Something like twenty Lord's Prayer and twenty Hail Mary?"

Sylvia understood the point of his joke.

"No! Never! It wasn't necessary. The one related to our kiss was the biggest I've ever had," she confidently answered.

Sylvia is a virgin, Mendel concluded, through the topic "penitence," not knowing, at the time, if he should be calm or worried about it.

The romance, since established, had had a healthy side effect on Mendel's routine. His domestic life and his religious attachments, instead of cooling off, were even stronger, as a way of convincing himself that having an affair with a gentile wouldn't affect either his marriage or his Judaism. On the contrary, he was giving more attention to Faiga's intermittent reports. He would patiently listen to her complaints and demands: the bathroom plumbing, the tile that couldn't be found, a warped door...

He had bought the new car and started driving with pleasure; it was different from driving a 34 Ford smelling of gasoline. They hadn't been going away for the weekends, so they reestablished the habit of traveling to Petropolis.[86] Disregarding his romantic raptures, Mendel was a perfect husband, a good provider, and more than ever dedicated to satisfying his wife's minimum wishes. In the style of King Solomon, he was wisely able to divide himself between the two women of his little urban kingdom, supplying the material necessities of one and the sentimental necessities of the other, while keeping his balance as a "fiddler on the roof."

Among the additional care measures, concerned about Faiga, he had asked Sylvia not to use her "Fleur de Rocaille" during their meetings, avoiding the delicious French perfume vestige in his suit or in the car. Sylvia was embarrassed, but concealed her female pride and bore herself with no complaints; it was part of the price for developing affection for a married man, not to mention the situations in which she had to promptly hide when a friend from the Jewish community showed up.

Moishele enrolled in Law School and started dating. By coincidence, or fate's lack of imagination, or maybe both, he was going out with a girl from a very Christian family. At the same time, the father and son relationship was wonderful. But the idea that difficult times lead to better days isn't always true; sometimes it's the opposite. With greater or lesser intensity, each one had his/ her own share of adversity.

Vicentina noticed Mendel was changed, but she couldn't feel the presence of a bad spirit; if there was a spirit intervening, it would be a good one, because she had never seen him hum-

---

86 Also known as The Imperial City of Brazil, in the state of Rio de Janeiro, 50 miles from the state capital.

ming and whistling like that. Before, he had been very parsimonious, and now he was talking to everyone in the house, sharing his happiness. He told Vicentina he would buy her a piece of land in the suburb; slowly, he would build her a house. Vicentina celebrated. A house! Something impossible for someone who a few decades ago had slave ancestors living in *senzalas*.[87] She suspected some unusual motivation was behind his generous promise.

His weekly meetings in the synagogue, were taking place as always, there were no suspicious looks or insinuations; he was keeping his secret intact. If one of his friends heard about him and a young and beautiful lady, he would put up with occasional ironic compliment: "*Sheine Meidele!*"[88]

Back on his feet, Sylvia's boss went to the synagogue for the first time to pray and thank the Almighty for his good health. He was smiling and happy, sharing obvious truths: "Money is nothing, health is everything! All diamonds in the world are not worth the moment the doctor releases you from the hospital!" Mendel had to keep his nerve while greeting and hugging his friend Abraham. They talked about business, and Abraham revealed another grace he had received:

"Everything was great at the shop; my manager reported everything from the first day I was absent; she wrote all down, not a small detail was missing. Even the sales increased, Sylvia is worth her weight in gold!"

Mendel felt a bit proud while listening to such compliments related to his girlfriend.

Abraham even joked:

"If I weren't married, I would ask her to convert and marry her."

Mendel kept the joke:

"And if she didn't want to convert? And, based on the same right, requested you to practice her religion?"

---

87 Crude constructions where slaves lived.
88 Yiddish, meaning "beautiful girl."

Mendel couldn't imagine how provocative and premonitory his "absurd" question was. Abraham wasn't joking this time:

"Never! The Jews converted only during the Inquisition, to escape the bonfire!" And then he maliciously mocked: "Women are a different kind of bonfire... They don't burn."

Mendel, smart, pretended to be naive in order to get more information:

"Such a beautiful lady and still single, it's hard to believe..."

Poor Abraham rose to the bait:

"And that's not all, she had almost ended up in a convent, she was going to be a nun. I know her parents, they're very Christian, they're always in church and don't miss a procession. Sylvia is their only child, always under strict supervision; during all the time she's been working with me, I've never heard of a boyfriend." And added, with a sigh: "Such a shame!"

Mendel was paying maximum and well hidden attention to his words. He was more than curious, he wanted to know everything about her. He hadn't discussed family matters with Sylvia, he hadn't asked, so he wouldn't been asked.

Talking to Abraham he confirmed his previous idea of her: a lady with an outstanding character, a very strong connection with her family, extremely worried about her parents, someone with no social life. Sylvia's upbringing under strict values and church influence, discouraging male attention, deepened Mendel's certainty that everything had really started with her admiration of his work, and then evolved to fondness. They also talked about commercial issues and their competition, ending with personal predictions related to the price of gold and the dollar.

A man, around forty, came closer. It was Samuel, son of the already deceased Levy Goldberg. He asked both to come to the synagogue the next day, to form a *minyan* and say *Kaddish*. Mendel promised he would be there. As he observed a son organizing his father's *Kaddish*, he felt a strong pain, which had been accompanying him for a long time: He didn't have a son to pray the *Kaddish* when he was gone. According to religious rules, a stranger could do it, but it would be a prayer without sentiment, something mechanic, normally for a payment. Furthermore, who would hire this person if not a relative? He thought about Moishele. On that occasion, he talked to the Rabbi to know if it was possible. The Rabbi heard the story of his foster son, and said that any person, independently of religion, could make a simple payment.

Mendel shared his wish with Moishele and instructed him: After his death, he should hire a pious Jew to say the prayer on his behalf.

Moishele said he wouldn't forget. Mendel had not accepted his lack of luck. Many couples had been formed on that journey to Brazil; *I was truly good-looking,* he recalled, *I could have chosen any girl.* On board, there were so many, lonely, insecure, girls who didn't have a clue of what was to come on an unknown land; it had taken him a long time to decide, he found imperfections in them all. By the time he managed to decide, there were only a few options left, and he ended up with Faiga. *Nowadays, all my colleagues who found wives on that boat, Samuel, Isaac, Aaron, have sons who are already doctors, engineers...* He had attended countless *bris* and *bar mitzvah* ceremonies; but fate had punished him for choosing too much, and he ended up married to an infertile woman. *I am a Jew without parties to be proud of in front of the Yishuv,*[89] he lamented. *Faiga couldn't even give me a daughter...*

It was the first time Mendel thought about his wife with such animosity. He had always accepted his marriage fate; he wouldn't discuss God's purposes. In fact, this mind twist was nothing more than a psychological defense concerning his guilt, a feeling that bothered him occasionally, even more if considering penal law — at the time, adultery was considered a crime.

The anxiety to meet Sylvia at the beginning of the fol-

---

89 Hebrew, referring to the body of Jewish residents in a given place, originally in Palestine before the creation of the State of Israel.

lowing week dazed him. For the first time, they would ride the new car; he was free from the limitation of his old and noisy Ford. Sylvia wanted to go out for dinner, have some wine in a free environment, in contrast to their previous elusive meetings.

Mendel chose a strategic place, the Alto da Tijuca, where couples used to go by car; and it wasn't far from their houses in Grajaú and Lins de Vasconcelos.

The nervous tension concerning their first meeting in a romantic scenario had made Mendel forget he was a *kosher* Jew, a follower of the Jewish dietary laws. They were already on their way when he remembered that religious obligation wouldn't allow him to touch impure food, not in accordance with the rules established centuries ago. But it was too late; it was impossible to turn to the love of his life and naturally announce: "My darling, we have to go back, I forgot that because of my Jewish diet I cannot have dinner with you." It would be the end of the world, and he decided not to take that risk.

All he could do was improvising a solution: He ordered fish and potatoes. Some species of fish were allowed and others were not, depending on having or not scales and fins. The benefit of the doubt made him feel more secure; he wasn't going to ask the waiter about the physical characteristics of the fish. Concerning the potatoes, he would be fine; after all, they were immemorial Jewish food.

Sylvia chose the same. However, eating fish would imply ordering some wine, and Mendel realized he had no way out. The closest bottle authorized by the Rabbinate was miles away, in some specialized grocery shop. Without wine, the anxiously expected date would be like a ball without music; therefore, in the name of love, Mendel Rosenstrauch, who had already forgotten his *kippah*, broke the rules of *Kashrut*[90] by accepting the suggestion of a profane white wine.

The romantic ambiance, reinforced by tricky sips of wine, temporarily removed from his brain the three hundred and six-

---

90 Set of *kosher* laws.

ty five religious restrictions of the sacred books (there are 248 obligations). He evaluated: *Not even in a dream I would have the pleasure of such moment, in a place like this...* It was worth it. Nothing else mattered; he had nothing to fear. Later, calmly, he would search the *Talmud* trying to find a breach to excuse his secret adventure with a *shiksa*, a valid argument in defense of the questionable fish and the inappropriate fermented wine.

Acting as a teen, he accepted Sylvia's suggestion for dessert, just because of its name, "Romeu and Juliet."[91] Redundant, excitement was overflowing: *This night alone compensates, with interest, for my voluntary exile...* He had even forgotten that such "exile" had saved his life, taking him out of Poland just in time.

In bed, he recalled the way they had looked at each other, everything that had been said, each word of affection and each smile they exchanged, how they had sensually touched each other. Standing aside his Jewish world and traditions, Mendel had felt privileged, saved from threatening clouds. The emotions brought by his loving conquest had not affected the harmony at home. Dear Moishele's filial affection still made him feel complete, and commercially he had nothing to complain about.

However, the Kabbalist living inside him knew that the imponderable peeps in each corner, reminding him of an exquisite case he had heard, which was recalled occasionally, brought up in the community through gossipers' giggles, mainly through female gossipers. When Leybel Rabinovich — one of the most radical orthodox Jews and a synagogue habitué — died, two funeral notices were published, side by side: One with the Star of David, in which his family informed about his passing, and another with a cross, in which his "companion and sons" reported the unhappy news.

Not by a long shot had Mendel compared his case to Leybel Rabinovich's, the deceased being an example of extraordinary self-control and "multifamily" management. As an orthodox, always wearing his long black overcoat and round hat

---

91 Traditional Brazilian dessert containing white cheese and guava paste.

like a piece of charcoal in the middle of the snow, lateral braids and long beard, how could he have lived with impunity for such a long time, between two different marriage universes, his Jewish nest and a gentile family? Mendel felt envious of his sons in both sides, all men. His Jewish sons prayed the *Kaddish*, and the other family ordered the seventh and thirtieth day masses. If Leybel Rabinovich didn't end up in heaven, it would not be due to lack of prayers.

Mendel was not that skilled, but he had remained stable in his home and in the synagogue. Sylvia fulfilled him as a man. They weren't consummated lovers yet, but shared the viable intimacy between an almost nun and a hesitant sexagenarian Jew, which used to make them feel as teenagers. They were both terrified about a possible pregnancy.

13. The Widower

Living people are not inert as a portrait hanging on the wall, which tends to stay put until the color fades away. We're like pieces on a chessboard, constantly moved by what we call "fate," or simply felled by time, with or without an advance notice, leaves on the ground taken by the wind or by an unexpected broom.

Mendel was about to complete four years of dating when a piece of his chessboard fell. Faiga, who had been his daily partner since they met on board, died of a heart attack.

The widower was depressed for long months. Only Moishele was able to lift him out of lethargy. He took him to the synagogue and didn't allow him to stop his visits to clients, in an effort to avoid the interruption of his father's work, that he considered the best treatment. Mendel recovered little by little, and emerged from silence.

They visited a resort. When they returned, Mendel was ready to resume his former independence. During this period of darkness and abandonment, sparkles of life started removing the shadows of widowhood. Although he hadn't told Sylvia about Faiga's passing — he was sure Abraham had mentioned it to her —, the figure of the woman who mobilized his hormones was always present.

As he and Sylvia met again, everything concerning their

dating routine was the same: They went by car to the customary Tijuca Forest, and through a tacit agreement, they didn't mention Faiga. Their physical contact, though, did not remain the same; it was now ferocious, overflowing, due to the time they were apart. The adrenaline rush made them realize it was time to take drastic measures, freeing them from all their immature, incomplete and repeated rubbing. Breathless, they looked at each other and thought together: *We can't go on meeting like that!* In a surge of courage, Mendel suggested:

"I can rent a discreet apartment for our dates."

Shocked, Sylvia pushed him away, leaving his arms.

"I didn't expect you to act like that! I'm not a prostitute! Up to now, our affair was limited by our consciousness alone. I've already sinned for having a relationship with a married man, a common mistake for people in love; they understand the situation of their partners and come to terms with it. It's not easy to leave a loyal wife, to destroy a relationship of years, I had to be patient! Now, the poor woman is gone. You're a free man. You say you like me so much, and I like you! Are we going to keep dating like teenagers hiding from their parents? Our age difference doesn't matter at all, I think we can build something good and decent."

Her strong conviction surprised him. She was suggesting that they should get married. He started the car and accelerated.

Mendel considered their relationship unchangeable; it was comfortable enough. But he clearly understood Sylvia's "message": She wouldn't be his lover.

"We'll talk about it some other day," Mendel ended the conversation.

They were both quiet along the ride. They didn't even kiss goodbye as he parked in front of her house.

Mendel was literally between the devil and the deep blue sea. He had lost the woman who kept his life orderly, and now was on the verge of losing the woman he was in love with. Sylvia's simple suggestion, "let's build something more serious," made him panic. He was willing to resist and negotiate an alternative, but to marry a *shiksa*...

He fell apart. The pain was no longer related to the sadness of losing his wife, it was a kind of suffering related to the flesh, an imprisoned desire. But he wouldn't budge an inch. She should relate to him unconditionally; he agreed with a bachelor friend who used to mock the female obsession about getting married: "Women prefer having a husband over getting the Nobel Prize."

Looking for her in that situation would demonstrate weakness, basically meaning that he had accepted that "something more serious." The daily prayer and the ancient tradition against mixed marriages protected him from offending the mandatory practice of his people. *She will call, she will call,* he obsessively repeated all day long, every day. But she didn't.

Mendel was afraid of taking such step towards assimilation and isolation. He had heard about religious Jews who had married non-Jewish women and were acting as *goyim*, losing their Jewish identity. The biggest pleasure of an Ashkenazi, which he was, was speaking Yiddish, the Diaspora language spoken by his parents and grandparents. Many people in Ostrow wouldn't even speak Polish, the official idiom. Getting married to a *shiksa* was equivalent to a tacit excommunication, and, on top of that, it would mean losing his heritage.

Mendel wasn't capable of giving away his ancient identity. To resist the temptation that threatened his most valuable asset, he relied on an artifice: He took refuge in his memories, the remote images of his past. He gathered and contemplated all the photographs he had brought from Poland — father, mother, grandparents, uncles, aunts, relatives, all already forgotten. In each frozen melancholic look he identified a call, a warning, telling him not to abandon the Jewish Street, the *shtetl* neighborhood in Poland.

Gradually, with greater or lesser sharpness, he was randomly gathering episodes that popped out of his memory and of the faded pictures. That way, he tried to dissolve the image of the woman who made him burn inside; he couldn't throw away his *kosher* history, his legacy as a true Jew. But he felt it was a lost battle. Dominated by the "burning" sensations during the movies and the eager rubbing inside the car, he was just playing for time.

He laughed, as he recalled his strategy to get a toy or a piece of candy from his parents: He would run through the streets without covering his head. In Ostrow, no man, adult or child, was allowed to go around with his head uncovered, it was an offense to the *Talmud*. There was at least one small factory of hats and caps in each street. He kept on his imaginary and useless sentimental "trip." He recalled the herring, the fatty fish that, in Brazil, he would buy at a delicatessen, very well packed to avoid spilling. In Ostrow, when his mother asked him to buy some fish, it was completely different; they wouldn't wrap it, paper was a rare thing, something so valuable that the thin wrap of an imported fruit was worth gold — a true luxury, used afterwards for hygienic purposes. A newspaper was read by many families; later, it was used sparingly in the commerce to wrap merchandise: The herring was only "half" wrapped, with a strip of newspaper around it. From 1914 and 1918, the printed name of the Kaiser was seen many times all around the fish, leaving out the head and tail, from where the brine would drip, allowing Mendel to have a "snack." The fish's head was honorably saved for the head of the family, different from Brazil, where it's normally discarded.

Rabbi Herschel was the local miracle worker. A long and strange line formed in front of his tomb on each anniversary of his death, going from the cemetery to the synagogue. The Jews from Ostrow would make him written requests, asking for the cure of diseases, financial success, a husband to their daughter. All requests should be written in Hebrew, so the spirit of the Rabbi would be able to "read." Curiously, the majority of the population was able to read Hebrew, but not to write. Therefore, the students and teachers made good money writing personal requests on tables spread throughout the line, a real industry. The student Mendel would be a part of it himself, because, aside from attending a Polish public school, he also attended the *cheder* and he could speak and write Hebrew.

What about the Sabbath? Many businessmen in Ostrow complained, but relinquished to the double weekly loss: On Saturdays, they didn't open their shops in respect to the Jewish day of rest; on Sundays, they couldn't open them due to the official Christian day of rest. He could easily recall the illuminated interior of the synagogue and its beautiful decoration. As a boy participating in the choir, from nine up to fourteen years old on Saturday mornings, he was enchanted by the two big eagles painted on the wall, one on each side of the Ark, with two carved lions over it, supporting the Tables of the Law. On the opposite wall, there were frescoes of Rachel's Tomb and the Western Wall. He had never seen such beautiful synagogue anywhere, much less in Brazil.

The five-hundred year old temple was an impressive building, but its height was limited by a Polish law: It couldn't be higher than the Christian church. Something curious about that place was the existence of a barrel filled with water in the vestibule, so men could wash their hands on their way back to the synagogue after going out to urinate. Next to it, a long towel, permanently dirty and humid after so much use.

Once, hidden behind the curtain, Mendel witnessed an anachronistic flagellation act in the synagogue. Some few radicals still adopted this kind of punishment: The *Talmud* specifies 39 lashes on the eve of *Yom Kippur*, but the punishment he had seen has been "negotiated" between the tortured and the executioner, who got some coins in exchange for softer lashes.

And how could he forget teacher Milstein's story? Mr. Milstein used to make a living selling pictures of the Virgin Mary and the Child Jesus in front of the churches. As he had a strong Yiddish accent, he pretended he was mute, a disguise which saved his life when the Germans arrived. The Nazis never suspected that the painter of Christian Saints was, in fact, a Jew.

Living in Brazil, the abundance of tropical fruits emphasized the memory of their lack in Ostrow, mainly because, in Mendel's hometown, the so dreamed oranges were not available. When his aunt, who lived in France, brought them some, they sliced the fruit in precious pieces and shared among his parents and siblings.

This pilgrimage around a world that physically no longer existed was a barricade to defend himself from apostasy. While visiting Ostrow, Mendel had seen his synagogue burned to the ground, the demolished centers of religious study. All he had was the memory of things and faces that, with a lot of effort, he could restore. A twist of fate has saved Mendel's life and attracted him to Brazil, and he understood that it would be a betrayal to even consider the possibility of eliminating his ancient spiritual heritage, out of his future because of a woman.

His tenacious resistance to the forbidden passion brought him back to his faith's roots, and he thought he was safe. It didn't last long; actually, no more than four or five days, until a sensual shadow, in the known form of a female, started coming closer and closer, dragging him once again away from the ghetto. The instinct had overcome the devotion.

The unhealthy passion, besides the emotional and organic deficiencies, made him capitulate. He was the one to call first, a gesture that should involve some concession. Sylvia remained distant, not once she showed any possibility of reconciliation; but she respected him for surrendering. They engaged in a prosaic, mellow, predictable and somewhat ridiculous dialog, expectable when considering the reunion of two people in love:

"Sylvia! It's Mendel."

"How are you?"

"Missed you a lot..."

"Me too..."

"I've been thinking about us."

"Unfortunately, Mendel, I can't think of a solution for us, considering the way you want to conduct things. I've already told you that I am an only child. My parents are very strict, very controlling; for them I'm still an infant, it doesn't matter if I'm about to turn forty. As for us both, we think differently. The religion..."

Mendel interrupted her.

"This is what I wanted to talk to you about. I want you to listen to what I have to say… I'll do anything…"

Sylvia didn't allow him to finish the sentence:

"Say no more, I don't want another disappointment, because I like you a lot."

"Let's meet, same place, I'll pick you up."

"I'm not sure…"

"I insist."

"Right, I'll be waiting for you; I'm not quite sure for what, but I'll be there."

In fact, the desires of the flesh were guiding Mendel's words. On the way to the meeting, he psychologically prepared himself to the "clash." Not intentionally, like in the *Kol Nidrei*,[92] that, according to Jewish liturgy, nullifies the binding nature of its promises in advance, he would signal acceptance to Sylvia's dream.

At first, the many kisses and hugs calmed him down, relieved him of the imposed abstinence regarding the touch and smell of that desired body. Her eyes, however, were demanding something else, and he knew what it was. In full ecstasy, he had to come up with a concrete proposal, as promised. Even so, he relied on the typical Jewish weighing of pros and cons: *Marrying this woman, a practicing Christian, was out of the question; suggesting a place for future meetings had terrified her, a "prostitute thing," according to her. I don't want to either lose her or marry her; I must find something halfway, something that won't let her down.*

He wouldn't be able to resist the darkness of a final breakup, in case she remained inflexible, but marrying a *shiksa* would turn his world upside down. As he kept his strategy of negotiating little by little, a result of his great commercial experience, he believed that the final "prize" would be his. But he needed to play for time, make her wishful.

He got a deadline.

---

92 The opening prayer of *Yom Kippur*.

14. THE SECOND WEDDING

Mendel believed he was in control of the final decision, and "living together" would be his generous proposal. Magnanimously, he decided to expose his irrefutable trump card. This way, he thought, he would put an end to the issue. He took her to Confeitaria Colombo, a famous pastry shop, the perfect scenario. He ordered some tea and toasts, and, quickly, anticipating the joy of victory, he said:

"We'll live together in my house in Grajaú." He was staring at Sylvia, expecting a wide smile of approval.

She answered ironically, something he couldn't understand.

"That's wonderful! I was promoted. Now, I'll be your concubine."

Frustrated, Mendel argued:

"So many people live like that... It's even better than being officially married!"

But Sylvia didn't allow this "debate" to go on. Even before having the tea and the toasts, she considered the conversation was over, and requested:

"Take me home!"

It was all back to square one. Dazed, Mendel needed more time to come up with a short poem or something, but he had a hard time finding it in his almost exhausted repertoire. When Sylvia got out of the car, instead of good night, he heard a sentence that sounded like she was condemning him to the gallows:

"Mendel, I want to get married, spare me the fake jewelry!"

Speechless, he observed her walking away. *Those forms, that gracefulness...* He felt the pain of losing her. But what could he do? According to his values, he had reached his top possibility with his last proposal. Sylvia's counterproposal should be the natural outcome, if she weren't a Christian and he weren't a Jew.

Once again, a long period of uncertainty and suffering started. He wasn't able to take her out of his mind, even while he was reading his prayer book. He couldn't work. On many occasions, with his clients, he made mistakes while counting the pieces. If it weren't for Moishele, who normally accompanied him, he would have suffered great loss.

Mendel was barely eating; he lost so much weight that he looked like a seriously ill person. Worried, Moishele wanted to hear Vicentina's opinion. His mother was discreet:

"It's not a spell! If it were, it would be easy to remove. This is a powerful passion, something very dangerous at his age. Mister Mendel needs help, talk to him man-to-man."

After much insistence, Mendel told Moishele the whole story, how he met Sylvia, the romance, even before he became a widower, and how things were at the moment. He could either get married or forget her once and for all, what he had already tried, without success.

Moishele, mature enough, asked him if he had tried to meet other women; perhaps, that way, he would be able to forget all about her. Moving his head from side to side, Mendel answered:

"All I've been doing is having dinner at the houses of widows Fany Bushinsky picks for me. But in each of these dinners, in which, by the way, I barely eat, everything goes awry: I can't help comparing them to Sylvia, and I end up feeling worse than before. I came to the conclusion that I can't live without her, but she insists on the fact that we must get married."

Moishele understood the kind of "illness" he was going through. He was lovesick, as Vicentina said. And he gave him his opinion:

"Why don't you marry this woman?"

The light shining in Mendel's eyes denounced that Moishele said all he wanted to hear. He expected some rejection in the community, but Moishele's encouragement brought him closer to his beloved woman; in his mind, instead of painfully missing her, his mouth "watered" as he imagined her naked.

Moishele advised him:

"Have a civil wedding, no religion involved."

Mendel hugged him:

"Thank you, my son!"

Certain that he would get a positive answer from Sylvia, Mendel restarted the phone harassment:

"Sylvia, I really need to talk to you."

"Mendel, acting like that you only make things worse, our situation has no solution, why should we keep hurting ourselves?"

"I've been thinking a lot, and I think you're right, can we talk personally?"

Sylvia noticed that Mendel's words were somehow different; and, after all, he was the one calling, after her loud and clear refusal on the day they went out for tea. Mendel was showing up with something "new" she wasn't sure about, but she needed to find out. Was he finally considering getting married? She needed that answer. Otherwise, she would keep her principles.

They met at a square bench, and after a few compliments — "You look so beautiful!" —, Mendel didn't waste time:

"I thought about everything you told me; we can't go on as two high school students, it's ridiculous. I agree. We are two free people who like each other, it was so hard being away from you during these days; so, I think we should get married, if you still want to take me as your husband."

Extremely moved, Sylvia kissed him.

"Of course I do!"

During long minutes, embracing each other, they remained silent. But it was time to be objective. Mendel, sovereignly added:

"And due to our religious differences, we'll only have a civil wedding."

Sylvia abruptly stepped back.

"Without God's blessing?"

Disarmed, under a lot of tension, Mendel used his last argument:

"It will be plenty of God's blessings if you convert to my religion."

Only listening to the suggestion of abandoning her Christian faith to embrace Judaism stirred up all her wrath:

"Never! Not even if my life were at risk, and the Christians proved that in the Roman Arena, when they were devoured by lions." She also provoked him: "The Jews, yes, they converted to Christianism to escape the bonfire during the Inquisition!"

Then she gave him an ultimatum that he hadn't expected to hear, even if he had lived for 110 years:

"I'm glad you've mention conversion, because I'll only marry you if… yes, if you convert to my religion, if you accept Jesus Christ as the Savior."

Mendel panicked. He knew Sylvia well enough to realize she was serious about it. He felt as a betrayer of the *Torah* simply by being there, intimately connected to someone who was demanding his spiritual "suicide." Feeling nothing but repulsion, he bluntly said goodbye and left, with large steps, as if he were running away from a tempting Lilith.[93]

At home, he locked himself in the prayer room, put his *tallit* on and prayed louder than usual, as he wanted to chase away the demon himself. He was no longer thinking about her

---

93 The name of a demon in ancient Assyrian myths. In Jewish tradition, she was Adam's first wife, sent out of Eden and replaced by Eve because she would not submit to him.

as his beloved partner, he felt ashamed for reaching that point. *Convert myself to Christianism! It's absurd! How will I pray for my deceased relatives on Yom Kippur? How can I live in a house without the* Sabbath, *without Pesach?*[94] He copiously cried and begged for forgiveness.

This episode made him even more attached to his religion. Not even once, he considered the fact that he had also asked Sylvia to convert to Judaism. A primary reaction made him look for Fany Bushinsky, the matchmaker. It was his turn to insist on meeting available Jewish women, to do anything he could in order to forget "that Christian."

Fany Bushinsky promptly answered his request, and presented him her marital catalog, so he could choose a fiancée among the recently included faces. There were even twin sisters newly arrived from Romania, and Fany enthusiastically recommended meeting them:

"Both are very beautiful, I haven't showed them to anyone yet, you'd better hurry up; if you don't like one, you can get the other!"

Mendel, however, didn't like either of them. They were really pretty, red-haired and freckled just as the deceased Faiga. He didn't want to spend the rest of his life with a copy.

The matchmaker didn't give up, she kept taking Mendel to dozens of Sunday lunches and dinners. The lonely women in their forties and fifties were truly interested, but he couldn't choose one; and, this time, he ended up gaining two pounds. Two or three counted on beauty and financial support, but Fany Bushinsky's campaign didn't get any results, and she had already been through all her existing catalogs. She could bring him two or three photograph albums and nothing would work, there was an insurmountable obstacle: The comparison with the image of another woman, which was all over the future fiancé's body and mind.

Mendel wanted Sylvia more and more each day, more

---

94 Hebrew word meaning "Passover"; the holiday celebrates the deliverance of Jewish people from slavery in Egypt.

than ever; he had become, once again, a prisoner of that law-breaking passion. And as it happens to all people who are obsessed, he was unhealthily missing his lost object of desire, and was, again, tormented by an uncontrollable crisis related to the deprivation of sensuality, which, as any type of addiction or dependency, emerged with more intensity, demanding immediate satisfaction.

Out of control, acting irrationally, he started stalking her. He would follow the streetcar she used to take until the final stop, just to make sure there were no competitors. Hidden, he placed himself next to her house at the time of the Sunday Mass, and felt relieved that only her parents accompanied her. Only then he could calm himself down; there was no other man in her life. There was no need to rush in.

He was gathering courage to take the most dramatic step in his life. He wasn't going to kill himself, suicidal Jews are dishonorably buried in the back of the cemetery, next to the wall. He was going to convert to Christianism, not to escape a condemnation, but to open the doors of the vaginal Sesame. History itself registered the conversion of the Protestant Henry IV to Catholicism, as a condition to take over the kingdom of France. Why couldn't he? He answered himself with the well-known citation: "Paris is well worth a Mass!" With Sylvia, there would be many masses, and she was worth much more than Paris...

Mendel resisted as much as he could. He felt he wouldn't be able to find a woman such as Sylvia in the "market"; he would no longer wait for the useless blind dates arranged by Fany Bushinsky. He would pay the price. In case excommunication was featured in the Law of Moses, he would be "excommunicated" from the synagogue.

It's a known fact that a circumcised Jew can leave Judaism, but Judaism will never leave him. It's also common sense that voluptuousness and loneliness are capable of removing a simple religious label.

Mendel talked to Sylvia about his decision. She knew it was out of love, an extreme measure that she, personally, in his place, would never take. But she didn't want him to accept Christ "paying lip service," under pressure. And she made herself clear:

"I'm happy to know that we'll be able to get married under the church's blessings, but I also know that our relationship won't last if you convert by a mere formality, only to marry me."

Mendel submitted himself:

"I'll do whatever you want, there's nothing more important to me than being with you."

Sylvia was constantly around Jews. Working at a jewelry shop, she created great affinity with the people from that segment, most of them followers of the Mosaic faith. She liked being around them. Because of that, she was aware of the importance of the *Torah*, and imposed her conditions:

"I know and admire your religion, but every Christian must try to save those who haven't truly found Christ. I accept marrying you, but only if you're sure you won't be a Jew on the quiet."

With unrestrained anxiety and euphoria, disregarding the seriousness in her words — that, in fact, he barely listened —, Mendel unwound:

"I've already told you I won't convert to escape a bonfire, but to get into another..."

Sylvia smiled, and was ironic:

"So, marrying me is a bonfire?"

They embraced and kissed; that's how they got engaged.

Mendel was perfectly aware of the step he was about to take and its consequences: He would be known as "*goyishe* Mendel"; he would suffer from the undisguised rejection of the community in general and would be despised among the orthodox. But he knew he couldn't live without her. He would become a Christian, but, as the Jewish actors who interpret the role of a Priest, he would live as a character. He would say the Lord's Prayer, confess, commune, make the sign of the Cross, kneel down whenever he had to; he would say he accepted Jesus. No one would notice that, even away from the synagogue, even inside a Christian temple, deep inside he would remain the Jew he had always been.

While the church members were praying, his lips would, inaudible, pray the *Shema*: "Hear, O Israel!" At home, he would escape Sylvia's supervision and find some time to pray.

He told Moishele and Vicentina that he was getting married. Both were happy and congratulated him, after all it was about time to start over; but when he told Moishele that, due to his fiancée's demand, he would convert to Christianism, the young man was perplexed, disappointed. He was proud of his Jewish father. Although, being an agnostic, he did not have a religion of his own, time and coexistence had turned him into a Jew by symbiosis, as he used to take psychological and philosophical roots in the Jewish tradition. Nevertheless, he decided to show Mendel only solidarity and support.

Mendel thanked him, barely hiding his embarrassment. And asked him, basically prophesying:

"Moishele, don't leave me; almost everyone will walk away from me, but I know you'll always be by my side, come what may." Very moved, both cried.

But Vicentina, an expert on life and human nature, felt that it was time to leave that house and her friendly rosebushes. She interrupted that serious moment to tell Mendel how happy she was for him; and said that, feeling happy and grateful, she was coincidentally going to retire. By the time the new mistress arrived, she would already be living at the house her boss gave her.

Later, away from Mendel, Moishele wanted to hear his mother's opinion about Mendel's decision.

"I'm sure he found a good woman, but they won't have kids to soften the shock caused by changing his spiritual direction; the faith he inherited from his parents and ancestors will not leave his heart..."

Time would prove, once again, that Vicentina was right.

Moved by his exacerbated lack of emotional control, Mendel wanted to rush the wedding. His religious beliefs, at this point, were not so important, undercover deep inside his conscience. Due to high anxiety, he avoided questioning the conditions "imposed" by his fiancée, a tireless advocate of her faith — a kind of Roman apostolic pact, a total submission to the dogmas and liturgies of the Church. They would live in a Christian house, abolishing the Hebrew symbols and habits. Sylvia herself would be the guardian, making sure all Christian duties were complied, and, by the bed, they would have just the New Testament.

A premature juvenile enthusiasm made him agree with everything; and she was merciless. She asked for proofs of his sincere resignation from the Jewish faith. He could no longer wear his *kippah*, go to the synagogue, keep the Sabbath and follow a *kosher* diet... And, above all that, he would carry a Cross on his chest.

Mendel even reinforced his "apostasy," and surprised Sylvia by reciting the Beatitudes, which he knew and enjoyed since the day Moishele had showed him the beautiful parable of Jesus learned in Religion classes. However, despite his pathological happiness, it took him some time to recover after Sylvia established:

"Start by removing the *mezuzah* from the door!"

It was a hard test. Mendel obeyed. His hands were shaking, but he unpinned it. This first great and practical desertion of the Laws of Moses made him feel mortified, and Sylvia made sure she was there to witness such painful act. He was aware of the symbolic power of that little object with a ritual prayer inside. Whenever he hesitated, the beautiful face of the woman next to him motivated him to go on, until he removed, using pliers, the last support of the charm. Submissive, he handed it over to Sylvia, as if he was delivering the head of John the Baptist to Salome. Sylvia made sure not a single trace of his former faith would remain. The *menorah* was also banned, as well as any object containing the six-pointed star; but she kept the decorative samovar Faiga brought from her hometown.

Two months passed by. In May, Sylvia took him to Priest

Felix to be baptized, and a few weeks later the wedding was held at the parish church.

They were living in the house in Grajaú; in accordance to her faith, the newlywed asked the Priest to bless their home. Mendel, paralyzed, inhaled the incense from the thurible, and was touched by many drops of Holy Water. On the main wall in the living room, in front of the dining table, a big print by Marc Chagall gave place to the Sacred Heart of Jesus, which dominated the environment.

They traveled to Europe on their honeymoon. In the Vatican, they attended a mass by Pope Pius XII. Mendel wanted to see Michelangelo's "Moses," but Sylvia, more radical than the Church itself, didn't allow him. Similarly, in Florence, she crossed David's sculpture out of the itinerary. They also traveled to Lourdes, in France, and to the Sanctuary of Fátima, in Portugal.

Concerning the daily routine at home, Mendel also accepted the gastronomic conversion. The *kashrut*, the set of Jewish religious dietary laws, was revoked, and the *challah*, the *gefilte fish* and the *beiguele* erased from the menu. On the dining table, Sylvia introduced the codfish, the kale & potato soup, the stew and the "nun's belly," a typical Portuguese dessert. Every time she served pork, Sylvia would pay close attention to Mendel, making sure he would eat it.

The crucifix on the headboard didn't cause a stir. Mendel was used to that: As a goldsmith, he had handled many golden and silver crosses. Moreover, meticulous Mendel argued with himself: *Christ was a Jew; as myself, He didn't even witness the establishment of Christianism.* And he whispered to the crucifix: *Yeshua,*[95] *this is not Your place...*

Counting on resilient balance, Mendel was managing a happy and calm couple's life. The religion adopted for external use fulfilled his wife's expectations and wasn't able to cross the Talmudic shield in his heart. Not considering mystical differ-

---

95 Hebrew name for Jesus.

ences, there was love between them. Sylvia was an excellent housekeeper and took good care of her husband.

She didn't need it, but she kept her job at Abraham's shop; and Mendel didn't sell his soul, he kept a secret fortress against the "domestic Inquisition," a balm which daily relieved his pain for abandoning the synagogue with melancholic proselytism.

In an old desk, inside a silk white bag printed in blue with the Star of David, he kept his *kippah*, his prayer book and his *tallit* given by his father when he left home to come to Brazil. Every day, while his wife was out, Mendel would lock himself in what used to be his prayer room; he religiously covered himself, put his skullcap and said the *Shema*. He was showing *Adonai* (the Lord) that he was still the same circumcised man, that he wouldn't worship the Golden Calf, that he knew He was unique. He didn't break the Alliance; it was only a ghost, not him, saying those impure prayers.

His fleeting moments with *Adonai* depended on a single key, which he carefully kept in his wallet in the left pocket of his suit. One day, however, his fragile wall went down, his secret "synagogue" crashed to the floor, not due to any tyrannical event or enemy's wrath, nothing like that. It was a trivial incident, very common as people get older, but it had a devastating effect: As Mendel locked the drawer, he absently forgot the key in the lock.

Such key was a novelty in the room. A drawer that is constantly closed conducts to indifference, it's something not to be used... and that's it! It was as if it didn't exist. But if suddenly a key showed up in the lock, no human curiosity would be able to resist, simple as that...

A turn to the left was enough, and Mendel's "little temple" collapsed, early in the morning, while he was still asleep... As Sylvia was leaving to work, glancing at that room, she was able to uncover his secret. The telltale finding revealed to her that Mendel, in fact, was nothing more than a "new-Christian," a Christian just for show. She had in her hands the evidences of his heresy: the *kippah,* the *tallit,* the S*iddur*[96] and the *phylac-teries.* Judaism was still part of his life. He had been baptized, but had only pretended to accept Jesus. Four centuries ago, he would burn up in the bonfire.

Sylvia started her punitive action immediately. She picked up the bag, using her fingertips, and gave it to the maid, ordering her to burn the whole thing, and rushed to work. Back home, she would give Mendel an ultimatum. She didn't want to run the risk of having a converted and excommunicated husband.

As he used to do "illegally" every morning, after taking a shower and getting dressed Mendel would say his first daily prayer. He looked for the key in his wallet and couldn't find it. Scared, he ran to the prayer room, and there it was, shoved in the lock. He felt the sort of relief people feel when they find something truly important they thought was missing. He belabored himself for being so unmindful and had a bad premonition.

First, he checked if the drawer was locked. Then, very nervous, feeling his old tachycardia back, he slowly turned the key. As he opened the drawer, he was in shock: It was empty, the bag with its precious content was gone. It was not hard to find out what had happened: While opening that forgotten drawer, closed for so long, his wife, motivated by natural curiosity, saw the intrusive white fabric bag and took it.

Nervous, Mendel ran around the house, uselessly checking all drawers and cabinets. Breathless, he went to the kitchen. Miss Lurdes, the maid who had replaced Vicentina, was helpful:

"Do you need anything, Mister?"

"Have you seen a white bag?"

"With a blue star?"

"Yes, that's the one."

"I've seen it. Mistress Sylvia gave it to me this morning and asked me to burn it and throw it away."

---

96 Jewish prayer book for everyday use.

Mendel's heart was beating threateningly fast.

"And where is it?"

Miss Lourdes pointed at the backyard:

"It's there, burning!"

Mendel ran outside and found his *kippah* and other sacred objects still burning. Out of control, with an animalistic cry, he knelt in front of that tiny *"pogrom"* and shouted at the sky, begging for forgiveness — "a thousand times, forgive me!" —, while he burned his hands, trying to pick what was left of his sacred objects covered in ash. Literally out of his mind, he held what was left of the objects against his chest and ran through the hall to the living room, counting on the merciful look from the sweet Rabbi following him.

He was on the street. With no destination, lost, he was wandering. Then he disappeared, taken by time...

Moishele and Sylvia desperately looked for him everywhere. It was useless. Sylvia, hearing from Miss Lourdes what had happened, and how disturbed Mendel was when he saw his sacred objects burning by her request, even considered he could have done something extreme; but there wasn't a body to confirm it. Moishele, however, knew Mendel would have never killed himself, he knew about his father's Judaism.

15. OLAM HA-BA[97]

They had never given up looking for him. Moishele, now a wealthy man, mobilized all kinds of public authorities, and hired private detectives, with no results. Days, months, years passed by...

Mendel became, little by little, a simple and nostalgic memory of someone who, if still alive, would be just the same as if he were dead. All they had left were sporadic questions: "Do you think he's dead? Where is he?"

They hadn't heard about him for a long time... actually, until the day Mendel had concluded his journey on Earth. He had been missing for over ten years when Moishele got a phone call from an elderly care home in the countryside. Someone told him that Mister Mendel had passed away and had asked a Masonic group to call him as soon as possible.

Moishele acted fast. He was in a hurry, he knew what Mendel meant by that "message." He quickly called the religious organization of the Jewish cemetery; he didn't even bother calling Mendel's brother Yacov, who had once said: "I don't have a *goyishe* brother!"

He decided to inform his wife of Mendel's passing at another time. Arguing about her rights, Sylvia would want to

---

97 From Hebrew, "the coming world."

bury him in a Christian cemetery, because, according to her, he was a Christian by baptism; but she didn't know Moishele had a document, notarized before their wedding, in which Mendel expressed his willingness to be buried according to the Jewish law. Sylvia gave up, but she felt cheated. It was all a big staging, her husband had never changed his faith, he had never accepted Jesus as the Savior; in his heart, he always secretly kept the six-pointed star.

Mendel had finally won the last of all battles to keep his loyalty to the *Torah*. He had been around clay idols, but had never worshipped them.

Only Vicentina and her son went to the cemetery. A religious man from the Congregation said the prayers mechanically, without expressing any kind of emotion. Contradicting the Jewish habit of not taking flowers to the cemetery, Vicentina was hiding a white rose in her hand, and she slowly placed its petals over his grave. Moishele whispered something from the "Prodigal Son": "He was dead, and is alive again; he was lost, and is found."

Someone proposed to say the posthumous prayers professionally in the synagogue. Moishele refused it. Mendel had always felt sorry for not having a son to pray his *Kaddish*, knowing that, when his hour had come, friends from the synagogue would suggest some stranger to do it, symbolically, for just a few days.

Mendel's death had happened just before Moishele's wedding. Cosmic irony determined that Moishele should fall deeply in love with a Christian girl, very religious. The arrangements were advanced, both for the party and the church ceremony, and the agnostic Moishele, indifferent to any formal religion, didn't oppose the demanded Christian baptism. He understood that walking down the nave wearing white, conducted by her father, to the sound of the nuptial march, was more than a simple bridal whim; it was a reason to live by, an inescapable dream.

On the day of the funeral, Moishele dreamed of Mendel. He even "saw" their first meeting during a rainy day, he as a new-born baby at the gate of the house in Grajaú, a story his mother has told him a million times. The dream also brought him the weeping and tight hug on the day of his graduation, Mendel's miracle. The next day, Vicentina asked him to take her to the house in Grajaú. She wanted to check the rosebushes, blooming as on that wet day in which a tall man, wearing a little cap on the top of his head and holding an umbrella, kindly opened the gate for her and the child she was carrying in her arms.

I received so much and gave so little in exchange, Moishele thought, without realizing that, actually, he had been a very dear son, who fulfilled an immeasurable emptiness in the heart of a good man, anguished for not having an heir who, one day, when he was gone, would say *Kaddish* for his soul, according to the Jewish precept.

Posthumous mercy, guilt, moral obligation, laymen and psychologists would say. Explain, who will? What happened was beyond ordinary human logic: The agnostic Moishele went to his fiancée's house, who lived with her parents, and told her that he really wanted to marry her, but not in the church; that he didn't want to convert being insincere, as he didn't accept the Christian baptism. He would only accept a civil marriage. All he got was a bunch of foul words, filled with racism, a characteristic of his bride kept completely hidden from him up to that point. The fiancée, as it normally happens, threw the engagement ring in his face, a ring he had made with lots of love, talent and art. For a second, he reconsidered. Then, even feeling hurt, he did not change his mind.

What is left is the amazing end of this whole story. Moishele was a descendant of free Africans forced into slavery on Brazilian soil; a history many centuries old that started in a wharf in Rio de Janeiro, on the day a group of Guinean chained captives arrived in Brazil. They brought in their hearts the pain of the exile, and, most of all, the African-based orishas in their souls.

Moishele gave in to his materialistic conviction — not to a metaphysical necessity, but to the call of a true filial emotion

— and talked to Rabbi Meyer about being converted. He got circumcised; and for eleven months, he went daily to the synagogue to say *Kaddish* for a righteous man, his father, Mendel Rosenstrauch.

www.ingramcontent.com/pod-product-compliance
Lightning Source LLC
Chambersburg PA
CBHW071311200626
46813CB00015B/1518